BEAST CHARMING

INTERSTELLAR BRIDES® PROGRAM: THE
BEASTS - 5

GRACE GOODWIN

GET A FREE BOOK!

JOIN MY MAILING LIST TO BE THE FIRST TO KNOW OF NEW RELEASES, FREE BOOKS, SPECIAL PRICES AND OTHER AUTHOR GIVEAWAYS.

http://freescifiromance.com

FIND YOUR INTERSTELLAR MATCH!

YOUR mate is out there. Take the test today and discover your perfect match. Are you ready for a sexy alien mate (or two)?

1

*W*arlord *Tane, Miami Event Center,* The Bachelor Ball

"WARLORD TANE, MAY I PRESENT..." Chet Bosworth, with his sparkling teeth and puffed hair, paused to look at the card he held in his hand. "The lovely Miss Patricia Wentworth from New York."

He shouted the announcement as if he were calling a horse race and was oh so excited to see who would finish first. I took the young lady's hand in mine and tried not to look intimidating.

"A pleasure," I repeated for the forty-seventh time. Leaning over, as I'd been instructed by Bahre's beautiful mate, Quinn, I dutifully held the female's small hand in mine and bowed at the waist. I believed meeting all the females currently in line would was a waste of time. I knew, even before Patricia had approached, that she was not mine. My beast knew as well. I had walked the room earlier, passed by each of the females in their fine gowns as they lined up, eager to enter and meet the beasts.

The young woman nodded her head and walked away, her expression carefully composed. I did not wish to disappoint any of the worthy females present but my beast would choose our mate, not I. And he was not interested.

"I do not know how much longer I can endure." I whispered the confession to Warlord Bahre where he stood next to me at the base of an elaborate staircase. The fucker's response was to laugh at me.

I discreetly elbowed him in his ribs, then turned to face the forty-*eighth* female being introduced to me.

By the gods, I had to endure several more hours of Chet Bosworth and his pontificating nonsense.

My beast and I were both losing patience.

As if on cue, Chet's conspiratorial whisper carried to both me and the young female approaching. "Hold your breath, people, as the alien, Warlord Tane, meets the next gorgeous woman in attendance. Celine Legrand traveled all the way from Gatineau, Quebec, Canada, more than sixteen hundred miles, to win this Atlan beast's battle-weary heart."

The young woman blushed at Chet's words. I greeted her, bowed, and released her with a gentle shake of my head. I did not need to tell these females they were not mine. They all appeared to be familiar with what had happened when the prior beasts on Chet's ridiculous show had found their mates.

If Celine were mine, she would already be in my arms. More likely over my shoulder so I could carry her somewhere private and pleasure her properly.

Without a live television audience.

Celine Legrand took a step back and then hurried away.

"Another strikeout!" Chet smiled directly into the camera and winked at the lens. "That's forty-eight in a row, my friends, but there are hundreds more waiting to meet our handsome prince. Is true love in the air tonight? Will one of these women be the answer to a broken-hearted beast's most fervent wish? Or will this lonely beast, this wounded veteran who has already been rejected by his own people, be doomed to face the executioner?" Chet twirled around in his black pants and long bright blue jacket, which nearly swept the floor behind him like a bird's split tail. His teeth were too large for his face, and his hair stood up on his head like thousands of small wooden sticks. He smelled like chemicals and false manhood and fear. He glanced from me to the camera and kept talking. "The gowns. The glamour. The suspense. We are still looking for our princess. Don't move a muscle. We'll be right back with more from the *Cinderella Ball* after a brief message from our sponsors."

Glamour? Gowns? *Suspense?* This was no game. Not for us, the beasts whose mating fever raged in our blood.

Did this idiot not understand what was at stake?

The blinking red light on top of the camera went dark, and Chet lifted a hand to summon one of his servants over to put more powder on his cheeks and nose. He shooed her away nearly as quickly, grumbling. "This is a dud. The whole damn thing. If one of these big aliens doesn't sniff his true love soon, we're going to have to move on to plan B."

Plan B?

I heard the low growl rumbling through my chest before I realized I had moved to stand immediately behind the human idiot. "What is this Plan B?"

He spun around, his mouth opening and closing like a fish's. "Um. Oh. Excuse me." He stepped back and I didn't press forward, afraid I'd give in to the urge to crush his skull. "That was nothing. I'm sure there is a woman here that can, you know, satisfy your beast."

"There is not."

His mouth went from opening and closing to gaping. "What? How do you know? You haven't even met—"

"I have scented every female in this room. My mate is not here."

"But—"

I turned to find Quinn and Bahre had followed me. "Oh no, Tane," Quinn said. "I'm so sorry. We can try again."

I shook my head. "No. Get one of the others to stand here. I am done." I took a step toward the exit. Stopped when Chet dared wrap his hand around my arm and pull me to a stop.

"You can't leave! We've been promoting this for weeks. We'll lose our sponsors. You're the main event, Tane."

"Warlord." I knew the beast had reached my eyes, felt the heat of the transformation pushing to break through. I had not given this fool permission to speak to me as a friend.

"Warlord Tane. Of course. My apologies." He was whining now. I glared at his hand, and he pulled his arm back as if burned. "Please. These women have flown in from all over the world for a chance to meet you and the others. If you leave, this will all be for nothing."

I'd break his heart with a fist through his ribs if he didn't stop talking.

"My mate is not here."

Chet sidled up to me like we were friends. We were not. "You know that, and I know that." He held his hand out and moved it in a slow, sweeping arc that encompassed the entire event space. "But *they* don't know that."

As I watched, some of the television crew's handlers, as Chet called them, stepped in front of the line of ladies waiting to meet me and began sorting them into small groups. The females varied in every possible way. Some were very young, probably virgins who would need delicate handling. Some looked at me like they wanted to ride my cock and knew exactly how to make sure we both enjoyed it. Some short for a human, some tall. All different skin tones, hair colors, sizes, and dress styles.

Quinn had kept her promise to me and the others. There were over three hundred eligible females at this event, dressed to enchant, to seduce. My beast hadn't shown even a flicker of interest so far.

Quinn stepped between me and Chet with a sigh. "I'm so sorry, Tane, but he's right. If you leave, the other women will be upset that they didn't get a chance to meet you. They won't understand. It would be a public relations disaster for The Colony, and I don't think we would be able to convince any more women to take a chance and attend something like this. If you leave, it might even discourage women from volunteering to be brides. Please, if not for yourself, stay for the others. Maybe one of them will find their mate tonight."

With a sigh, I looked up to where Kai and Egon stood several paces in front of me, acting as guardians and guideposts to the line of females eager to be introduced. They, too, inspected the human women gathered, looking for their own mates.

All the earthbound Atlans were present. Velik, the Atlan guard from the Interstellar Brides Processing Center here in Miami. Kai. Egon. Determined not to waste an opportunity, each governor from The Colony had sent six warlords each.

There were nearly fifty Atlan warlords at this ball. Two dozen Prillon warriors guarded the perimeter of the building, here at Warden Egara's behest. They were not Atlan, but there was nothing stopping them from finding an eligible, willing female to claim as their own.

The last thing we needed, according to the warden, was any kind of incident that would hurt the Coalition's image as Earth's benevolent protectors.

What had begun as Quinn's simple idea had turned into a media circus.

Warden Egara's words, not mine. She was here somewhere as well, talking to the women who would not be chosen, encouraging them to volunteer to be Interstellar Brides. The processing center could guarantee them each a match with a worthy Coalition fighter, be that a set of three Viken fighters, a pair of Prillon warriors, or an Elite Everian Hunter. And there were more: the cyborg survivors on The Colony. The Forsians. Hyperions. Xerimans. Alerans. All worthy males who had fought to protect the planets in the Interstellar Coalition. All looking for a female. Eager to claim a mate, to be matched by the most advanced psychological program in existence. Warden Egara could promise them a happy ending, a mate to protect and care for them. I could promise nothing.

"I will stay."

Quinn looked relieved. Chet Bosworth looked annoyed. Bahre's face was carefully blank, as was mine. I would not deny my fellow warlords, nor the Prillon warriors guarding the perimeter, the opportunity to mingle with so many willing females. Perhaps one of my brethren would be luckier than I.

For them, I would bow and greet over three hundred females.

By the gods, it was going to be a long fucking night.

I settled back into position at the base of the stairs, prepared to behave and speak niceties for the next few hours.

"I feel like a prized stallion on display," I grumbled, eyeing yet another camera crew perched on the balcony above us, filming everything for the rapt television audience.

Bahre chuckled from where he stood behind my right shoulder. "That's exactly what you are, my friend. You are the star of the show. If you leave, all of this will stop."

"So we have established." I turned to frown at his attire. "And why are you dressed all in black, like a shadow, and I am wearing *this*?" I tugged on the rigid cotton collar and fluffy white necktie choking me. "I'm no Prillon. I do not require a collar."

"You look amazing." Quinn stepped close to brush an imaginary piece of lint from the dark red shoulder of my gold-embroidered jacket. She smoothed the fabric. "That is a Victorian Ascot necktie. Don't mess with it. You are

playing the part of a fairy-tale prince. We've been over this."
Her smile was radiant. Beautiful. Her simple black gown
hugged every curve and perfectly accented her red hair and
fair skin. She was the perfect complement to Bahre.

If I could find a human female like Quinn to calm my
beast, I would be blessed indeed.

"Besides, every single woman in here is drooling over
you guys. All of you."

I looked around and had to agree with the lady's
assessment. I was not the only Atlan who had stuffed his
body into tight white pants, frilly white shirts, and the
stiff red jackets with gold buttons. The costume I wore
was made complete by golden ropes and tassels on the
shoulders.

When the television show's makeup specialist had
approached, I'd growled at the poor thing. I had stuffed
my body into stretchy white pants. Putting rouge on my
lips was out of the fucking question.

We all looked ridiculous. However, we deferred to
Quinn's advice. She assured us this strange attire would
please the human females, make them less afraid of our
large sizes.

We were all desperate enough to do whatever she
asked. Mating fever raged in my blood, as it did in the
others. We were running out of time.

Kai and Egon were similarly dressed, as were the
unmated Atlans sent from The Colony. The Prillons were
far luckier in their black pants and dark coats. As security, they were not meant to draw attention. The ballroom
opened to a high ceiling filled with two rows of crystal
chandeliers. Around the perimeter of the ballroom, a
second level, lined with arched balconies, provided the

perfect vantage point to watch over the dance floor. Standing beneath each arch, staring down at the gathering of humans, stood either an Atlan or Prillon guard, some crammed next to the large camera equipment the humans were using to record every movement, every word. *Everything.*

Thanks to Warlord Maxus, the Coalition Fleet had become aware of Nexus Six's and the Hive's growing interest in Earth. Prime Nial had ordered two dozen Prillon warriors sent from Prillon Prime to safeguard each human continent. An additional contingent of warriors had been installed at the Interstellar Bride's processing center here, in Miami, and at the other processing stations around the globe.

The human governments had been warned. Yet when we petitioned them to allow extra protection on the ground, they had refused. Prime Nial and the governors on The Colony had taken matters into their own hands. If Nexus Six had developed a special interest in Earth, ignoring the threat would not improve the situation.

Additional protection was in place whether the humans wanted to acknowledge us or not.

Chet's high-pitched whining interrupted my musings.

"Warlord Tane, may I present Miss Anja Kunkel of Hamburg, Germany?"

With a sigh I returned my attention to fulfilling my duties as host and main attraction and gently took the lady's delicate hand in my own.

2

*E*lena Garcia, *Parking Lot,* The Bachelor Ball

"WE'RE LATE." I took a step back and used the huge dumpster near the building's rear door to hide from view. The caterer and her servers hustled from their trucks as I tugged the bodice of my borrowed gown up over my chest. *Again.* The damn thing was too tight, pushing my breasts into embarrassing mounds while simultaneously threatening to drop away and expose them at any moment. One wrong move and I'd be flashing more than my smile.

"Are you sure about this, Elena?" Dominique asked. She was Abby's manager and public relations specialist. She'd been hired by Abby's father personally. Given an office in his building. Watched like a hawk. She would be in just as much trouble as I if things went wrong tonight.

"Yes. We have to. We have to get in, find her, and drag

her spoiled little butt out of there before anyone realizes who she really is."

"Damn it. I knew you were going to say that."

I grinned at her. "Unless you miraculously came up with an alternative solution in the last three hours?"

"You know I didn't." We both turned to survey the door again. "We are running out of time. She's probably been inside for at least an hour. You know trouble finds that girl like bees find honey."

"I know."

"You brought the invitations?"

"Yes. But neither one of us looks like a"—I checked the name on the invitation I had stolen from one of the offices at Gregg Media Group a few hours ago—"Katinka Friðfinnsdóttir."

"You butchered that."

"I don't speak Icelandic."

Dominique burst out laughing, and I had to join her. We were both darker-skinned than any northern woman would be, me with my Mexican heritage and her, not from her French father but from her Malagasy mother. Both of us had hair so dark it was almost black. Dark brown eyes. We didn't have a single Icelandic gene between us.

We also did not have invitations, so we couldn't simply walk in. Between the security detail and the mob of paparazzi out front, we didn't stand a chance of getting in through the front doors.

I sighed and blinked twice to clear my eyes as one of the biggest, scariest men I had ever seen walked out of the building to stand in the dim glow of the parking lot lights. He wore a black uniform that did nothing to disguise his size. A second man joined him, and they stood there, doing what looked like guard duty, at the back door. "Oh shit."

Dominque made a choking noise. "Oh my God. They're huge." She took out her cell phone, put the camera on, and zoomed in. Once she'd snapped the picture, she turned the screen to me. "And they're not human."

I looked closely. She was right. Their faces were close to human, but the angles were too sharp and their skin tones looked...off. One of the aliens was more golden than a good tanning bed could produce, and the other was even stranger, his skin shining like polished copper pipe.

"We can't do this. There's no way." She tilted her chin toward the aliens. "Not with those gorgeous aliens standing there. No freaking way."

"Gorgeous?"

Dominique rolled her eyes at me. "Shut up; you know what I meant."

I looked at the guards again. She was right. They were stunning, masculine, all muscles and stern expressions. They were hot. And they were men. Male aliens. Whatever.

"You go first. They'll let you in, and I'll just tag along." Men fell at Dominique's feet on the regular. I doubted these aliens would be able to resist her any more than a human. She was too beautiful. If I were a lesbian, I'd be obsessed with her myself. She was seductive without trying. Me? I was the opposite. Reserved. Quiet. Too honest. I never knew what to say or when to say it. I lived with the nearly constant hum of anxiety squeezing the air out of my body from inside my rib cage.

"No way," Dominique protested.

"You're gorgeous. You're single. You're all curves and sex in that dress. You look amazing. They'll take one look at you and let us in," I assured her.

"I don't know, Elena. Maybe we just let Abby pay the price on this one and go home."

"I wish." And I did. Abigail Elizabeth Gregg, heiress, social media star, and sad, lonely young lady, was a just-turned-eighteen-year-old ticking time bomb. She was beautiful, a world-famous heiress with no mother, several million followers on social media, and a vapid, shallow stepmother who spoke poison into daddy's ear. Abby was miserable. Angry. Hurting. The girl was an absolute mess, but we couldn't allow her to ruin her life just to get daddy's attention. The fuck-boy playthings she had paraded in front of her father since her birthday had been bad enough.

But an alien? He'd kill the poor man—alien—and sink the body in the swamp.

Then again, probably not. The alien unlucky enough to tangle with the billionaire's daughter would simply... disappear. Poof.

We had to get in, find Abby, and drag her out of there before anything terrible happened. I sighed and nudged Dominique toward the door. "Think of it as jumping the line at the nightclub. You do it all the time. You're hot. You're female. You're dressed to kill—" Her gown was simple, shimmering navy-blue silk that clung to every single one of her curves like a second skin. "I look like a walking wedding cake. But if you go first, they'll let us in."

"This is insane." Dominique was shaking her head as she reached for my hand.

"They're aliens. They won't have any idea what someone with that name would be expected to look like." I slipped my hand into hers, and we both took a deep breath.

"That's true."

"Besides, it was the only invitation I could find." I'd had to dig through office trash at the Gregg Media Building's complex to get my hands on Ms. Iceland's invite.

"This is a disaster waiting to happen."

"Trust me, I know." I squeezed my friend's hand and took one last look at my gown. "At least you look good. This dress makes me look like a walking marshmallow." I reached up out of habit and found my neck bare, again. "And I feel naked without my locket."

"The dress is gorgeous. *You* look like a fairy-tale princess. Or a queen on her wedding day. You should be wearing a tiara. Seriously. That dress is next-level brilliant. You know the designer is from Paris."

"So you said." I released her hand to tug on the gown again and double-checked to be sure the golden chain holding my locket was still securely fastened around my wrist. An antique locket would look odd with this dress. Dominique was right about that. But I never took it off. Ever. It was my most prized possession, handed down for four generations, and all I really had left of my family.

"Quit fussing."

"It's tight." This was the only dress that had even come close to accommodating my oversize curves. I steadfastly ignored the fact that the elaborate bodice was creamy and white and that my breasts looked like mounds of honey-flavored ice cream, each with an over-size dollop of whipped cream up front. One look at me and the aliens would be thinking about food, not sex.

The gown was more appropriate for a fifteen-year-old's quinceañera than a grown woman's desperate rescue mission. Glitter and sparkling layers of satin and tulle began at my waist and fell in multiple layers to my ankles. The skirt was so full I had been forced to turn sideways to get out of my bedroom. Worst of all, the fabric was creamy white, and I was a klutz. The gown would have something spilled on it within the first ten minutes, no doubt.

"This is going to be a disaster," I muttered.

"That's what I said." Dominique stood and lifted her chin, squared her shoulders. "When I get my hands on that girl, I am going to wring her little neck."

The expected echoes of ballroom dancing music rose and fell as the back doors opened and slammed closed. This kind of rescue mission was very much *not* part of my job description. Yet here I was, about to sneak into a building full of aliens. Honest-to-God *aliens.*

"Are you ready?" I asked.

"Hell, no. But let's go." Dominique adjusted her gown as well. Unlike me, she was thin and trim and perfectly proportioned—if a bit too tall—for the dresses we'd borrowed from the stepmonster's closet. Dominique looked perfect. Coiffed hair. Stunning jewelry. Artfully applied makeup. The rich, gorgeous caramel-colored skin she'd inherited from her Malagasy mother glowed next to her dark blue gown. And every time she spoke, her father's native French accent spilled onto her words just enough to make them sound exotic. The only thing I wasn't jealous of was her super-curvy backside. I had one of those, too.

I kept my eyes glued to her back as she sashayed toward the two alien guards. She didn't make a sound, but the aliens turned toward us the moment we gave up our cover and walked in their direction.

A hard pebble pushed through my soft-bottomed slipper, and I pasted a false smile on my face so I wouldn't grimace. We were both wearing flats because the gowns were too short for either one of us to wear with high heels. Stepmonster was barely five-three, and Dominique and I were both much taller than average. We didn't exactly blend, no matter where we went.

"Good evening, gentlemen. We are here for the ball." Dominique spoke smoothly, not a hint of uncertainty in her tone or her body language. She looked and acted like a queen who expected to be obeyed.

I waddled up behind her in my mountain of fluff and waited as the copper-skinned alien took the invitation from her hand and scanned it.

"This invitation is for one female only."

"Surely the single gentlemen inside won't mind if there is one more beautiful, available woman to choose from?" Dominique swept her hand toward me as she said the word *beautiful*, and I held my breath, waiting for them to tell us to get the hell out of here.

The two aliens looked at one another, and the golden-skinned man gave a slight nod of agreement. At once the copper-skinned alien stepped to his side and opened the door for us. "Very well. But you are not where you should be if you wish to get in line to meet Warlord Tane."

"Oh no? Where should we go?" Dominique put her

full-wattage smile on, and the Prillon appeared to be momentarily stunned. His golden friend cleared his throat.

"My lady, if you and your friend turn to the right once inside, you will see a corridor with a stairway at its end. Those stairs will take you directly into the lower-level ballroom." He locked eyes with Dominique, and suddenly paralysis appeared to be contagious.

I grabbed Dominique by the elbow and tugged her stiff body along as I moved inside. "Thank you."

"My lady."

I wasn't sure which one of the aliens had spoken last. I sighed with relief as the doors closed behind us and Dominique snapped out of her weird trance.

"Oh my God. I have to get me one of those."

"Those are Prillon warriors." I had recognized the sharp facial angles once we were close enough to speak to them. "They mate in pairs. You'd have to take two of them."

"Seriously?" She shuddered and a little giggle escaped her lips. "Even better."

I rolled my eyes. "Let's go before one of them hears you."

We hurried down the corridor toward the stairway the Prillons had told us about. The music swelled to fill the hallway, and I knew we were in the right place. We passed a number of carved archways in balconies that overlooked what I assumed was the main event down below. Huge aliens were in every single balcony, watching everything with scowls on their faces.

"Do you think they're expecting an attack?" I asked. "They look a little too serious."

Dominique ignored them and kept walking. "They're extreme alpha males, and there are a lot of women here. They are probably thinking about baseball and tacos so they don't have to walk around with erections all night."

"Tacos?"

Dominique was giggling again as we neared the top of the stairwell. She stopped just before we cleared the corner and peeked around the edge. She turned back to me. "Holy shit, there is no way we'll find her in that mess. There must be hundreds of women here."

"She has bright pink hair," I reminded her. "That will help."

"She dyed it yesterday. Didn't you see her feed? She went platinum blonde again."

"Great."

Dominique tilted her head. "You go down the stairs and mingle. Make sure you search behind all the nooks and crannies. There are pillars and decorations I won't be able to see through. I'll circle around to the far side of the balcony and search from up here." She pressed flat palms to her stomach, and I suspected she was trying to hold in the butterflies just like I was. "Look up every couple minutes, okay? I'll point you in the right direction if I see her first."

I would have argued, but my distance vision wasn't the best and I was wearing an old pair of contacts. Dominique could read a street sign from two blocks away. "Okay." I braced for the impact of music and people and...people. "Cell phone on?"

"Right here, ready to buzz the boobies if you need me." She patted the center of her gown, and I knew she had hidden her cell phone in her cleavage, as I had

"Same." I held her gaze. "Let's do this."

Dominique gave my shoulder one final squeeze before scurrying across the open stairway entrance, past it to the alcoves and balconies on the opposite side.

"You can do this. You can totally do this. It's fine. Everything is fine." I tried to talk to the terrified little girl inside me as I moved into place at the top of the stairs. The dance number swelled, the Prillons remaining on the periphery as a number of Atlans escorted females around the dance floor. The ballroom fell silent as the song came to an end. I lifted my gaze from the paisley design in the carpeting and watched as the people below milled about, chatting and laughing and drinking champagne. There were so many women. So many. And some of them had on dresses even bigger and more ridiculous than mine.

Thank God. I smiled in relief, so very happy to know I was not going to stand out like a fluffy swan in a roomful of sleek falcons. I allowed my gaze to wander over the rest of the guests. Mostly women, but there were tall aliens in black here and there, like the two we had met outside. There were also dozens of tall, muscled, ridiculously handsome men scattered around the room, each dressed up like he was Prince Charming.

So *that* was an Atlan warlord.

Shit. The television did *not* do them justice. I'd watched a couple episodes of *Bachelor Beast* out of sheer curiosity, but Chet Bosworth's voice made me cringe, so I hadn't watched more. Apparently I was not the only woman who thought they were gorgeous. Every single one of the Atlans I could see was surrounded by smiling, flirting, laughing women. All except one.

He stood alone at the base of a stairway directly opposite mine. As I watched, first one, then a second in what I realized was a very long line of women, was introduced to him. He dipped his chin politely, took the woman's hand, bent at the waist like he really was a prince.

Holy hell, he was beautiful. Tall and strong, like the rest, but he had dark, serious eyes that made me wonder what horrors they had witnessed. A chiseled jaw perfectly framed the most kissable lips I had ever seen. His brows were slightly darker than his hair. Trimmed to sweep across his forehead and curl slightly around his collar, his hair looked warm, gleaming like the jar of maple syrup in my pantry did when the light shone through the bottle.

He made me think of danger and sweetness in one tantalizing body, and I couldn't stop staring.

He bent low over the hand of another woman, touching her. Speaking to her. This one was slim and blonde and wearing a tight red dress that made her look like a Hollywood star walking the red carpet.

Shocked at the emotion churning in my gut, I fisted my hands at my sides and tried not to hate her. Like really, really hate her. Jealousy was a mean, merciless bitch.

That had to be Warlord Tane, the star of the show. Tonight's most eligible bachelor.

And I wanted him. For myself. Stupid. Irrational. Masochistic. Nothing good had ever come from me wanting a man. I had two former fiancés and a semi-retired vagina to prove that.

Tearing my gaze away, I looked for Dominique along the line of alcoves in the balcony. I found her in the designated place, leaning over the railing as she searched the crowd. She looked up and waved at me impatiently, mouthing the word, *Go!*

Right. Abby. I was here for a reason, and it wasn't to ogle...

I looked down into the ballroom, at the hundreds of moving bodies all surrounding the alien hottie who was this evening's star attraction. His eyes were focused on...*me?*

I froze. Stared back. What was happening?

He was staring straight at me.

No. That couldn't be right.

I turned to look behind me. No one was there.

A slight tremor made my hands shake as I turned back around to face him. He was gone from his place directly opposite these stairs. A wavelike movement pulsed through the crowd, and the guests parted, forming an open lane across the entire dance floor. He walked between them, his gaze locked onto something...

Was he leaving the ball? Going to the restroom? Did aliens even do that?

No. He was coming *toward me.*

Panicked, I looked up to find Dominique. She was shaking her head, moving her hand across her throat in the universal sign for *you're dead.* On her lips she mouthed the word *run!* over and over as the alien drew closer.

I should have run. Turned. Walked away. Anything but what I did, which was stand there like a statue as he came to me, the entire crowd of people going silent as they watched.

He paused several steps below me, his gaze focused,

intense, level with mine.

"My lady."

"Sir."

"I am Warlord Tane of Atlan."

That made me grin. I couldn't help it. Talk about stating the obvious. "I figured."

His answering smile made my heart literally skip a beat. It hurt.

He bowed low, actually dropping to one knee on the stairs. He was dressed for a medieval fairy tale. White pants, knee-high riding boots, a white shirt with a fancy collar that looked like it belonged in a historical romance, and a dark red jacket that hung past his hips. The jacket was thick, embroidered with golden thread, lined with golden buttons, and with golden epaulettes covering his massive shoulders. It was over-the-top. Ridiculous. So sexy I wanted to tackle him. The whole situation was like a dream.

"You are beautiful, more beautiful than I dared imagine." His voice was deep and melodic. Hypnotizing. I felt like I was in a trance.

Why was it suddenly so difficult to breathe? I took him in, every inch of him, as I tried to regain some sense. Only he could make those ridiculous, tight white pants look good. Then again, it wasn't the pants that made my pulse race. It was the thick, muscled thighs, his perfectly shaped hips I had no doubt led to an amazing backside, and his huge...

Oh my God. That was not a sock. Not. A. Sock. And it was growing.

He held out his hand. "Would you honor me with a dance?"

Say no. Say no. Say no. You have a job to do. A teenaged drama queen to rescue.

"Just one dance." I descended the stairs to place my hand in his. Skin touched skin. Heat raced up my arm like a jolt of electricity. My heart thundered. The faces of everyone else in the ballroom blurred. The floor felt like it shifted under my feet, and I nearly lost my balance.

His hand tightened on mine, helped steady me. My gaze locked with his, and I forgot everything else. I could not walk away from him right now. He was too tall. Too handsome. Too sexy. I had never, not once, *ever* had a man look at me the way he did now, like I was the sun and moon and stars, with totally focused, rapt attention.

Never would again. That would be my bet. I was too tall. Too big. Too curvy. Too smart. Too much sass. Too much of just about everything. Men ran from me; they didn't cross an entire sea of people to ask me to dance. Things like this just didn't happen. Not to me. Not in real life.

One dance. It would only take a few minutes, and I would remember this experience forever. Besides, I was dressed like a princess. Might as well give the gown a whirl.

He rose to his feet slowly, his body towering over mine when he moved closer. As he'd done with the blonde in the red dress, he bent low over my hand. But rather than stand at once, he lingered long enough to place a kiss on my wrist. "Anything you desire shall be yours."

One kiss and my nipples were hard as rocks, my barely there panties were wet, and I trembled. Not a bad opening line for an alien dressed up like a prince.

3

MY BEAST ROILED beneath the surface of my skin, fighting to break free. To touch her. Scent her. *Claim her.* Our mate.

Gods, my mate was beautiful. Her hair was nearly black, the strands shimmering like liquid darkness over her shoulders and down her back. Her skin looked soft and smooth, the full mounds of her breasts an invitation above the tight bodice of her gown. The dress was unlike any of the other females' in attendance, clinging tightly from her waist up, then exploding in a shimmering, glittery confection from hips to ankles. The costume was extravagant, elegant, and I knew when I held her close, the folds of her gown would wrap around my legs like a lover's caress.

I wanted that. Even more, I wanted her naked and

yielding to my beast and his cock. I needed my mating cuffs around her wrists, my seed in her body, my scent on her skin.

I *needed.*

My hands shook and I prayed to the gods she would not notice the show of weakness, the desperation my beast felt to be near her. I led her to the center of the room. The dancing area cleared, as I had known it would, and I was eager, proud to introduce my bride to the world. Show her off. Mark her as mine. Stake my claim. This beautiful woman must have suitors. Any other male, from *any* species would know, after this night, that to harm her would mean their death.

Not that I would allow any male to harm her. She. Was. Mine.

The music that swelled to fill the room came from a gathering of humans sitting in chairs. Each of them held an instrument with strings; some played little pipes held to their lips. I stood opposite my mate and held out my arms as I'd been taught by the dance instructor Quinn had insisted upon.

I'd hated every moment of the lessons. Considered them a complete waste of time. But as my mate stepped into my arms, her body fitting perfectly to mine, I realized she knew this human tradition. Expected me to know as well.

At my nod, the group of musicians played what I'd been told by Quinn was a slow, dreamy waltz that she assured me was very romantic for human females and would make my mate fall in love with me. I guided my mate around the dance floor, her body pressed to mine, her gown tangled with my legs, the entire world watching.

Nothing had ever felt more perfect...

Chet Bosworth's annoying voice broke the sanctity of the moment. "Oh my God, people. Oh. My. God! What is happening? Did Warlord Tane just find his mate? Who is this mystery woman? I have to tell everyone at home, I don't see her on the guest list. I have access to all the eligible young ladies' pictures, and I don't see her. Is she some kind of Cinderella? Where did she come from?"

Chet prattled on, but I tuned him out. Standing near him, Bahre was beaming with pleasure as he watched me dancing with my mate. And Quinn? She was literally bouncing up and down, tugging on Bahre's arm, losing her composure.

Was she *crying*?

Her reaction made no sense to me. I was the one who had found my mate. Surely, if anyone were to lose their self-possession, it should be me.

Females were strange, emotional beings. And now I was blessed to have one of my own.

Looking down, I swirled us in a circle and focused solely on my mate. My female. The woman I'd been waiting my entire life to meet. Her dark brown eyes were roaming over my face, pausing on my lips. Moving on. Coming back to them. Did she hunger for me as I did for her? I should be a gentleman. I did not wish to frighten her with the intensity of my need for her. But my question was spoken before I could talk myself out of it.

"Do you want me to kiss you?"

"That transparent, am I?" Her smile was soft and inviting, her voice barely more than a whisper. But I heard her. I would always hear her. "I'm sorry. I shouldn't be staring."

My beast rumbled in my chest as her feminine scent climbed its way inside every cell of my body.

Leaning in close, I gently settled my lips against the edge of her ear so no one but my mate would hear my confession. "I need to kiss you. I need to touch you. I need to hear you say my name."

"Tane. Your name is Tane." Her breathless whisper made my body shiver, my cock swell to the point of pain. "I'm Elena."

"Elena." By the gods, her name was as beautiful as she. I breathed her in, pressed my lips to the skin below her ear, along her jaw where the delicate curve met her neck. With the press of my lips, she melted in my arms, her body supple and relaxed as I led her around the dance floor.

"Do you know what I am?" I asked.

"An alien?"

Her blunt response made me smile. "I am an Atlan warlord."

"I know. And I shouldn't be doing this right now. I really shouldn't. But apparently you are irresistible."

I laughed, the sound as much a shock to me as to Chet Bosworth and his television crew.

From his place on the stairs, Chet spoke into the television camera, his back to me as he continued prattling on. "Did you hear that, ladies and gentlemen? Have we ever heard a beast laugh? I'm not sure we have. Whoever this mysterious woman is, she appears to have captured Warlord Tane's complete attention. The waltz is almost over. I'm going to move in closer to the glorious couple so we can speak to her directly. Ask her a few questions. I want to know more about her, and I'm sure all of you do, too."

Chet of the large teeth and tall, stiff hair was not wrong about one thing: Elena held my *complete* attention. Her confession to finding me impossible to resist pleased me greatly. My beast preened with satisfaction at her words. She was mine—ours—and she was honest as well as funny. My heart felt lighter already, the burdens of war and battle, of my time as a captive of the Hive, all of it faded in importance to this moment. This woman was my reason for everything. Fighting. Killing. Suffering. Surviving. All for her.

Chet Bosworth spun around in a dramatic flash of movement, and I purposely twirled my mate in the opposite direction, moving as far across the dance floor as possible as the music came to an end. The moment it stopped, I took Elena by the hand and pushed through the crush of females craning to get a look at her.

Desperate to be alone with her, I glanced up to find two of the Atlan guards watching me, waiting. I gave a nearly imperceptible nod, and they moved at once, calling upon the others to intercept and redirect the guests as I gently led Elena to the edge of the room, then into a small lounge I had discovered when inspecting the building earlier. There was not much to the room, two oversized chairs with a small table between them, a false fireplace that displayed an image of fire on a screen rather than the real thing, and one small sofa barely large enough to hold me.

But it was private. And the door locked.

Elena walked calmly with me as I pulled her into the

room. Two Prillon guards moved to stand in front of the door with a nod, a promise of protection. Several steps beyond them, one in every direction, Atlan warlords took up position as well. No one would get past them. My friends. These males who understood the significance of the moment, of Elena. Her existence would either save my life or, if she deemed me unworthy, end it.

I was prepared for either outcome. I was tired. So fucking tired of fighting the buzzing of the Hive in my mind with every waking breath. Tired of being alone. Tired of fighting the war and worse, my beast. He raged, even now. The beast's pain was mine. His rage? Mine. Each day my beast became more difficult to control. Restless. Furious. In pain. Constant, never-ending agony.

Mating fever had its claws sunk deep into both my body and my mind. I could not hold back the beast much longer. To be Atlan was to know this may one day be my fate. To lose control. To succumb to mating fever.

To be executed by my fellow warlords for the protection of all.

"Wait! Warlord Tane! Wait! I have a couple questions. Who..."

Chet yelled as he ran toward me, toward Elena, and was stopped dead by two fierce warlords who stepped into his path. I grinned and slammed the door. Locked it as Elena watched like a curious little bird peeking out at the obnoxious male from behind me.

"I don't want to talk to him," Elena said.

"He will not come near you." I cupped her cheek in my palm as I made the vow, her instant sigh of relief my reward as she leaned into my touch, trusting me to care for her. Shield her. My beast preened within, pleased with her acceptance of our protection.

Fuck Chet Bosworth, his television crew, and his annoying, conspiratorial tone of voice as he described every move I made as I made it. *Tane is leaning over. Tane is walking. Tane is scanning the guests. Tane is scowling.*

Tane is locking the fucking door and will crush your small, human skull if you dare try to interrupt.

With the door now closed, my mate pulled away to walk deeper into the room. I leaned my back against the door and admired her movements. She was graceful. Feminine. The gown floated around her legs like sparkling clouds. The bodice hugged her form and pushed her breasts up into full mounds I could not wait to taste. She was lush and curved, soft, so that I would sink into her warmth when I fucked her. She would be my home now.

"Elena."

She spun around to face me, her hands gripped tightly in front of her waist. "Why did you bring me in here?"

"Because I need to kiss you and I do not want Chet Bosworth to broadcast our first kiss to the entire world."

"Oh." Her cheeks flushed and she licked her lips as if nervous. Or undecided.

"Did you change your mind about our kiss?"

"No." Her gaze locked with mine, part challenge, part desire. I moved without conscious thought. To her. Closer. Protective. Obsessed. Elena watched me with wide eyes but did not move away when I lifted my hands to her cheeks and gently tilted her chin up.

"Are you sure? I do not wish to pressure you." She was

mine. I had time. I would not rush her or frighten her. Not even with a kiss. I wanted her frantic with need, as desperate for my touch as I was to touch her.

Our gazes locked and I held myself paralyzed, waiting for her response, her dark eyes deep wells of emotion I would happily drown within.

"I have something I need to do, but no, I didn't change my mind."

"Thank the gods." My lips were on hers before I'd finished speaking. Tasting. Taking. Exploring her mouth as her unique flavor exploded on my tongue. She tasted of chocolate and berries, of sweet, submissive female. She opened for me at once, her lips clinging to mine. She lifted her hands and buried her fingers in the hair at the base of my neck, pulling me close as her body trembled in my arms. Her passion was gasoline on an already burning fire, my beast raging now, nearly impossible to control.

Elena tore her lips from mine. I refocused my attention on her neck. The swell of her breasts. Her hands remained in my hair, tugging me this way and that, making demands I was only too eager to meet. I used one hand to lift her full breast from the top of her dress. Her dark nipple drew me like a beacon, and I feasted on her body as a soft moan escaped her throat. Her head fell back as I lavished first one nipple, then the other with attention. They were hard peaks against skin softer than I could have imagined.

She gasped. "I shouldn't be doing this."

"You are safe with me. I will take care of you." I backed her toward the chair until her knees bent and she sat, facing me.

"It's not that." Her gaze lifted to me, her dark eyes slumberous and heavy with her need to come. To be fucked. To feel me inside her. The call of her wet pussy, her welcoming heat, her body's craving for me filled the air in the small room and drove my beast wild.

I dropped to my knees before her, eager to taste her core. Feast on her body. Taste what was mine. Very gently I placed my hands on her ankles as I held her gaze. She was panting, the pulse at the base of her throat beating a rapid pace. "I want to touch you."

"Okay."

Moving slowly, I caressed her legs, moving my strokes upward from ankle to knee, to the tops of her thighs, to the sweet swell of wet heat between her legs. She gasped, her knuckles white where she gripped the arms of the chair. The glittering, puffy skirt was bunched between my chest and her body, my arms hidden from view beneath the beautiful, feminine layers. Staring at her over her gown, I knelt before my goddess, my mate, and prayed she would accept me here. Now.

"Do you want me to stop?" I held perfectly still as I gazed into her eyes. She didn't look away. She hid nothing from me, not her arousal nor her nervous shivering. Her body responded to my touch so quickly, so easily. Once I learned what pleased her, she would be like lightning in my arms, burning hot and fast. Eager for my touch. My kiss.

My cock.

"No. Don't stop."

The moment she'd spoken, I slid two fingers deep inside her hot, wet core. She moaned, her legs opening wider, accepting my touch. Demanding more.

"Oh God."

"Not your god, your mate." There was a slight bit of fabric I assumed was meant to cover her pussy. A thong. I knew this, as did the other warlords, for we had made it part of our purpose since our arrival on this planet to learn everything we could about human females. I moved the bit of lace aside and applied my thumb to her clit as I fucked her with my fingers.

I expected her to lean back on the sofa and surrender to her pleasure. Instead she reached for me, tugging frantically at my jacket, pulling me forward so that I covered her torso with my chest even as my arm disappeared beneath the mountain of sparkling gown.

"Kiss me," she demanded.

No need to be told twice. Taking her mouth, I did not relent. Not when her pussy went into spasms around my fingers, not when she cried out. I took her mouth and swallowed her cries, her pleasure, took them into myself and let them sink deep, calming the beast.

I pushed her over the edge again, her taste addictive. Her cries made my cock weep with pre-cum, the hard length aching to fill her.

I could not truly claim her here, now. Once unleashed, my beast would be impossible to control. And he would want time. Privacy. I wanted her naked for days, my cum dripping from her body as I took her over and over again. Cuffs on her wrists. My beast would demand her complete and total surrender, arms over her head, naked body open and on display. Pussy ready and wet, eager and willing to accept either my mouth or my cock.

I would give her both.

Her body arched and shivered as I held her down

with my palm pressed to her mound. My fingers remained unmoving, buried deep in her core. She shuddered. Panted. Her fingers tugged at my hair but stopped. Moved down, over my chest. She yanked on the buttons, gave up in frustration. Reached lower.

"Goddamn it." Her dress blocked her intent. Was she reaching for my cock? She shifted her position until she was half sitting, her breasts thrust toward me in an offer I could not resist.

Claiming her nipple, I worked my fingers inside her until she moaned in surrender and fell back to rest in the chair. Soon her hand would be on my cock. Perhaps her smart mouth would surround it as well. One day soon her wet, pulsing pussy would wrap my cock in pure fire.

The thought made me shudder.

She shifted again. Reached for me. Fell back. Made an odd, adorable grumble. "Damn dress."

I lifted my head to look at her flushed face. By the gods she was beautiful like this. In my arms. Looking at me with desire in her eyes. Want.

Acceptance.

"What do you need?"

"You."

I froze, terrified to hope. This was too easy. Too perfect. "I am here."

"You're not inside me. I need you inside me. Now."

My cock throbbed with pain, too hard, too full, as if the damn thing had heard her.

"You want me to fuck you? Take you? Fill you with my cock?"

Her soft moan made my pulse race even before her words made something inside my chest explode in an agony I'd never felt before, the pain new and unfamiliar. Torment and ecstasy both.

"Yes."

She was fucking perfect. Mine. Fucking mine.

Standing, I took a step back and ensured she watched every move as I reached for the buttons holding these tight, white pants to my frame. Slowly I released my cock. The eager fucker sprang toward her like an animal, hard and long and starving for her. Her gaze drifted over me, and I allowed her a long minute to look her fill. "Is this what you need, princess?" I fisted my cock in my hands and worked it from base to tip as she devoured me with her eyes.

"Yes." She fumbled, unable to move, buried beneath the dress. Her breasts hung over the bodice, full and lovely and red from my attention. I could not see her pussy, her thighs, but I knew she was hot and wet and ready for me.

"I have an IUD, but—"

I saw the hesitation in her. The worry. "What worries you?"

"Do you... you know? Do you guys have anything I need to worry about?"

I leaned over her, taking her mouth in a kiss. "Worry about what kinds of things?"

"You know." She panted as I kissed her again. And again. Ran the tip of my tongue along her lips. Gently. Slowly. Exploring her as she seemed to struggle for words. "Sexually. Transmitted. Disease—"

Ah. She was worried about human illness. "No, we have no such diseases."

"Must be nice." Her gaze locked on to mine. "Kiss me again."

I leaned close and held perfectly still, my lips nearly touching hers. "With pleasure. Anything you desire shall be yours. I told you this."

"You can't be serious."

"I am. Anything, Elena."

"That's crazy. What if I asked you to kill someone?"

"Is someone threatening you? Are you in danger?" I stopped breathing as I waited for her response. She looked away as if nervous. "Tell me." I would kill anyone who threatened her. Destroy them. Tear them into tiny, bloody pieces.

"No. It's just, this is not normal. Not for me."

"I am happy to be your exception." I kissed her slowly. Deeply. I needed her to feel what she meant to me. Life. Love. Obsession. Dedication. Passion. No one and nothing mattered to me but her. Not anymore. "I need you, Elena."

"I can't...I... Shit." Her dark eyes stared into mine, unguarded. Vulnerable. "I need you too. I want you inside me. And hurry. I don't have much time—"

I had no sane thought as I pushed the long skirt of her gown up and knelt in position between her legs. The hardwood floor barely registered under my knees as I pulled her hips toward me, felt my way to her core. I aligned my cock with her pussy and then—

Scorching heat. Wet welcome. Bliss.

My mate.

Mine.

A roar rose within me as I claimed my female for the first time. She made soft, mewling sounds and buried her hands in my hair. She dragged me to her with relentless and demanding hands. My beast paced within, impatient to have the mating cuffs on our wrists. On hers. He fought to be free. To fuck her. To have his cock in her body, to claim her as I did now.

"God. You're huge. So good." Her whispered words made me nearly explode with satisfaction. My mate was pleased.

My beast scoffed. She had yet to see *huge*.

Moving slightly, she dropped her hands to my chest, adjusted her hips, and my cock suddenly slipped forward with the new angle, buried deep inside her in one smooth motion.

The moment was like a dream, surreal because I could feel her body around me but could see nothing but clouds of glitter and fabric between us. I touched her petal-soft skin beneath the skirt, ran my palms along her bottom and thighs, held her where I needed her to be as I filled her. She was tall for a human, tall enough that I could enjoy the taste of her shoulder, her neck, her breasts. I set my hips to a pounding rhythm as I sucked her nipple into my mouth.

"Yes. Yes. Yes." She clawed at my shoulders.

Yes. I agreed.

I fucked her then. Hard. Fast. Until she came all over my cock. Until she wailed her pleasure. I did not stop until I filled her with my seed. Claimed her. Marked her with my scent. Until I knew every Atlan warlord and Prillon warrior on patrol would know she was mine. Completely. Under my protection. My mate.

4

THREE ORGASMS. *Three.* That was a first. Most guys I'd dated in the past barely cared enough to get me to one, and some never made the effort at all. But not Tane. I felt...amazing.

Another first? I'd never had sex fully clothed before. He was still inside me as the aftershocks in my core pulsed around his cock. His lips pressed to my neck, covering my sensitive skin in lingering, soul-melting kisses that made me feel precious. Adored. Having clothes on made it more decadent somehow. Wicked. I felt like a goddess—a naughty, very satisfied goddess.

In fact, I wouldn't mind staying right here to enjoy his attentions all night.

I allowed my head to fall back as far as it would go, hoping Tane would cover every bit of exposed skin with kisses. His hair was so soft. I was petting him, running my fingers through the dark strands as if he belonged to me. I squeezed my inner muscles just so I could enjoy the shiver that raced over his body when I squeezed his cock. I loved that I had such a strong effect on him. I should do it again...

Oh God. Shit. What the hell was I doing? I was supposed to be helping Dominique find Abby. Besides, this was not me. I did not do things like this.

Ever.

The dress, the music, Tane himself. Everything must have gone to my head.

Having sex with a complete stranger? Going at it like a wild animal in a... What was this room anyway? A library? *That's* what I was doing. Hot, hard, take-me-now sex that would have sent my mother—God rest her soul —to her knees to pray a full rosary before lighting a candle in a desperate plea for my sinner's soul.

The fact that I hadn't even taken off my clothes now felt like a mistake. This was all a mistake. I'd lost my mind. Temporary insanity, and I had no one to blame but myself. My breasts were out, resting on top of the bodice like a pagan offering. I'd *asked* him to kiss me. *Demanded* he have sex with me. And now I was lying here like a puddle of melted ice cream as he licked and kissed and tasted my skin. Worse? I never wanted him to stop.

This was bad. So, so bad. I had no idea where Dominique was. Or Abby. My part of our mission to save Abby from herself was a massive failure. I'd let them both down for an alien I'd met, what? Half an hour ago? I was in a borrowed dress that was now going to have not only my juices but alien *semen* all over it.

The Stepmonster, Abby's new stepmother, would literally *kill* me if she found out.

She couldn't find out. Never. I'd have the dress cleaned tomorrow by her high-dollar specialist. I'd even pay extra for the express service. She would never know... as long as we got Abby home safely and kept her off the news, away from all social media, and no one knew she'd been here, especially her father.

The warmth in my blood turned cold at the thought. That man was merciless when it came to his only child.

Shit.

With a sigh I felt all the way to my toes, I gently pushed Tane's lips away from my shoulder and struggled to sit a bit straighter. He took the hint at once and slipped from my body. The moment his hard length left me, I felt empty, like I'd lost something more than his flesh. Like the only connection I had to him was gone forever.

He settled back on his heels, watching me, his legs folded beneath him as I tucked my heavy breasts back into the tight bodice of my ball gown. They were sensitive now from Tane's attention. The skin flushed. My nipples sending streaks of sensation to my core as I forced them to rub against the gown's lining. Tane watched like a man possessed, like he wanted to rip the gown from my body and shove me to my hands and knees on the floor. Pump into me from behind. Tug on my hair and...

"Stop." What was wrong with me? I'd truly and completely lost my damn mind. That wasn't what Tane wanted. That fantasy was all me. All. Me.

"I am unclear what you wish me to do." Tane had sorted his own clothing, put his impressive length away and fixed his jacket. He was back to looking like Prince Charming. Handsome. Noble. Irresistible.

I wanted to kiss him again. Instead I bit my lower lip to prevent myself from saying something stupid.

"My lady?" He looked confused. Concerned. I didn't like seeing that expression on his face.

"I'm sorry. That wasn't directed at you. I was talking to myself." Had he really just made me come all over his cock and then gone all prim and proper? Called me a lady? I was the daughter of a paralegal and a mechanic. I was from a working-class neighborhood. I was no shy virgin, and I had never been waited on or pampered a day in my life. A lady? Hardly. I was a working woman with a job, student loan debt, and a car payment I could barely afford.

Breasts back where they were meant to be—along with the cell phone I found next to me on the cushion—I cleared my throat and tried to think of something *not reckless* to say to him. Came up with...nothing. Every thought in my head sounded stupid to me right now. Embarrassing. How was I supposed to act? I'd never done this sex-with-a-stranger thing before. And thank God it was just sex. I knew these Atlans had their mating cuffs, like giant wedding rings that went around the wrists. Tane didn't have those with him. Hadn't mentioned them, which meant he was waiting to give them to someone else. This really was a one-night stand. I was in the clear. Why that thought hurt, I refused to think about. For now I just had to get out of here and try to forget this had ever happened.

Fat chance I'd forget the best, hottest, most amazing sex of my life. But I would try.

I shoved the skirt of my gown down to cover my legs and looked around the room, searching for a mirror. I had to go back out there, had to help find Abby and drag her out of the building before she ruined her young, spoiled life.

And mine. And Dominique's.

Couldn't do that if my hair looked like a rat's nest.

I scanned every wall, every surface. Damn. No mirror.

I settled for running my fingers through the long, straight strands, thankful I'd been in too much of a hurry to try a fancy hairdo tonight. I had my straight hair down. It was smooth and easy to comb, falling just past my shoulders. No fuss, just the way I liked it.

Tane was watching me, the expression on his face impossible to read. He looked like he wanted to say something but either didn't know what he wanted to say, or he was afraid to say it. I understood the sentiment. I had plenty on my mind, and I was terrified to speak a single word.

What, exactly, had just happened between us? He'd asked me to dance. I'd stared at his lips like I would die if he didn't kiss me. He'd kissed me and then, had I been satisfied? No. I'd begged him to have sex with me.

I was in so much trouble. Why didn't I have better self-control? This wasn't like me.

As my body cooled, my mind cleared and I began to hear the ambient noises around us. The music coming through the closed door. The ticktock of an ornate grandfather clock that stood against the far wall, its golden pendulum swinging back and forth with precise, perfect timing. The sound ratcheted up my anxiety on every beat. Tick. Tock. Tick. Tock.

I glanced at the face of the clock, at the delicately carved hands that showed the time.

Five minutes to midnight? I'd been with Tane for well over an hour? It had seemed like fifteen, maybe twenty minutes.

Oh. My. God. Dominique was going to strangle me.

A scuffle sounded from just outside the door.

Speak of the devil. I recognized her voice ordering one of the very large aliens I assumed still stood outside to get out of her way.

"Katinka? Are you in there? I found our little sister." Dominique's question was accompanied by what I knew was the knocking of her knuckles on the door in an exact, demanding sequence I had heard many times before.

"Coming!" I called out before I thought better of it. Tane looked confused.

"Katinka? Is that your true name?"

"Oh." Damn it. What would the alien security team do to me if they found out I had sneaked into the ball with a stolen invitation? I was not supposed to be here. "Yes."

Tane looked like I had stabbed him in the heart with an ice pick.

"I mean, no." I wrapped my right hand around the locket and chain I'd fastened around my left wrist, seeking comfort. Guidance. Strength. The familiar shape soothed me enough to speak clearly. "My friends call me Elena. Please, I'm Elena."

That seemed to appease him, and he stepped forward to take my hand in his. He looked down to study the locket as the door burst open. Dominique and Abby stumbled inside in a hurricane of silk and perfume.

"Sorry to interrupt." Dominique looked from me to Tane, paused as if shocked by how freaking gorgeous he was, then turned back to me. "We gotta go." She inclined her head toward Abby, who looked stunning—and extraordinary—in a deep red gown that hugged every inch of her body like a second skin. Her hair was piled on her head in an elegant sweep that made her look well beyond her eighteen years. She was a grown woman, fully formed, and determined to defy her father in every possible manner.

She was also ambitious, calculating, and had known exactly what she was doing sneaking into the event. She claimed she wanted the publicity. She didn't need it. She already had several million followers on her social media accounts.

She *wanted* to anger her father. Get his attention. Which was not a good idea. At least not like this. George Richard Gregg III hated aliens like my mother had hated snakes, with a blind, irrational, and unrelenting fear. Abby's father was not a man who experienced that emotion often. As a result he was determined to use his multibillion-dollar media empire to thwart the Coalition's mission on Earth in any way he could.

If he found out Abby had been here, at the aliens' Cinderella-style ball, he would come *unhinged*. He would probably have a stroke on the spot. I would be fired immediately for failing to stop her. Dominique would be fired for the ensuing public relations disaster. Abby would probably be miserable, cry in her room for a week, scream at her father for being a hard-headed ass, and gain several hundred thousand new followers.

Dominique and I, however, wanted to pay our bills.

Eat. The little things. If we lost our jobs? Not good. Not good at all.

I gave Abby the best version of a mom glare I could manage and held her gaze until she dropped her head.

"I'm sorry, E."

"You're going to get us in trouble. You know that, don't you? You're going to get us fired." I wanted to rage at her, but I couldn't bring myself to do so. Abby, like me, had lost her mother when she needed her most. I knew that pain, recognized it in her.

"I said I was sorry."

Tane hovered at my side, clearly unsure what the hell was going on. I wasn't going to tell him. That would defeat the goal of getting Abby out of here with no one the wiser. Fantasy over. Time to go back to reality.

"I'll yell at you later." I looked at Dominique, who nodded in agreement. "Did anyone see her?" I asked.

"I don't think so."

"Did she talk to the press? The paparazzi outside?"

Dominique was shaking her head, but Abby answered. "No. No one knows I was here. No one noticed me."

"Thank God. Let's go before our luck runs out."

Dominique turned back to the door, followed by Abby. I fell in step behind the girl, Tane on my heels. I glanced over my shoulder to see what the hell he was doing. He stared back, eyes unyielding.

Okay. So he wanted to walk me out. Dressed like that. He was, after all, the star of the show. "You need to stay here, Tane. They'll see you."

"I will not leave your side."

My heart did a strange and painful flip-flop beneath

my ribs, but I was already shaking my head. "Everyone knows who you are. They'll be looking for you. We have to get Abby out of here without being seen."

He paused to consider, then nodded to two of the large aliens who had been standing guard. They looked at me, studied me, and I realized they must have heard us. I racked my brain trying to remember if I'd screamed or moaned or said anything to Tane when we were having sex. I had. All of it. And they'd heard. All these aliens had heard *everything*.

And I hadn't thought I could get more embarrassed. Wrong. So wrong.

"Clear the path. Take us through the utility corridors. Allow no one to see them."

"Yes, Commander." The aliens hustled to do as Tane had instructed, and we were being escorted out, completely surrounded by alien warriors—or warlords or whatever. Each one of them was more than a head taller than me. And I wasn't short. Neither was Dominique, who was just shy of six feet tall.

We hurried through nearly empty hallways that were clearly used to load and unload supplies for the kitchens. The scuffed tile looked like it had been beaten to death by pallets, forklifts, and heavy boxes, countless footsteps and carts on wheels. This was a far cry from the elegance and glamour of the main ballroom, and I was relieved. I felt like I could breathe.

Maybe, just maybe we were actually going to get Abby out of here without a national incident.

Dominique was in front, telling the two nearest her where we'd parked.

A set of double doors opened to reveal the darkness

of night. The parking lot was quiet. Nearly full. The ball seemed to be going on despite the fact that the main attraction had disappeared. With *me*.

Me. Who would believe that? No one.

"Hurry. I'm parked over there." Dominique tugged at Abby's arm, pulling her along like the naughty child she'd acted tonight.

"I want to take Daddy's car. I told him to wait."

"The limo? You came here in the limo?"

"Yes. You know I don't drive."

Jesus, Mary, and Joseph. The girl was asking for trouble. Begging for it. "Text Roger and tell him to go home," I ordered. "Now."

"But—"

"Now. You are *not* walking around front to get into a company car." I placed my hand on her shoulder and squeezed. "Are you *trying* to get us fired?"

"No. I'm sorry." Tears gathered in her eyes as she pulled her cell phone from her clutch. Her fingers flew across the screen. I almost fell for her act. Almost.

"Stop." I held out my hand. "Give me the phone."

"What? No!"

Dominique came up behind her and took the phone before Abby could protest. Quickly she looked at the screen. "Damn it! She just posted our location."

Too late. Already we could hear the scrambling and shouting of the paparazzi as they ran around the building to find us. Tires screeched. Headlights appeared, bouncing up and down as the vehicles racing around the building drove like maniacs to get to us.

No, not to us. To her. Abigail Elizabeth Gregg. Heiress. Social media star.

Pain in my ass.

"Run!" I grabbed Abby by her elbow and shoved her in front of me. Dominique was in front of her. She grabbed hold of Abby's opposite hand and was pulling her along.

Car doors slammed. Voices shouted.

We weren't going to make it.

I dared look back and nearly stopped dead in my tracks. Tane stood in the middle of a wall of alien warlords, blocking the paparazzi's view and their path to us.

They were saving us, giving us a chance to escape.

We made it to Dominique's SUV, and I opened the back passenger's door to shove Abby inside. The windows were tinted to keep out the sunshine. No one would be able to see Abby or take her picture once I closed the door.

I slammed the door on her distraught face and looked back over my shoulder to search for Tane as Dominique ran to the driver's side and opened the door.

There he stood. He was amazing. So tall. So strong. So freaking gorgeous. I didn't want to go. I wanted to stay. Talk to him. Maybe have some more fun, this time with our clothes actually off. Where did he live? Here? On Earth? Didn't some of the aliens live here now? Or would he go home to his planet when he found the woman he wanted to put his mating cuffs on? Would he take *her* to Atlan? That's where the warlords were from. Did it even matter? Why should I care? We'd had sex. Great sex. But he hadn't said a word about making things permanent. No mating cuffs. No declarations of undying devotion or demands to stay with me forever. I'd watched *Bachelor*

Beast, watched Warlord Wulf shout the word *mine,* carry Olivia off to a dressing room, and have his wicked way with her on live, national television.

Tane had not used the word *mine.* Not once. I knew what that meant.

My cheek was wet. I lifted a hand to wipe away fresh tears and wanted to smack myself. Why was I crying? This was stupid. I was being ridiculous.

"Look out!" Dominique's warning came too late. A harsh grip circled my wrist, trying to pull me away from the SUV. The man was almost exactly my height with slicked-back, graying hair, a nose that looked like it had been broken more than once, and a scar running through his bottom lip to the base of his chin. He smelled like cigars and cheap beer. He yanked at my arm in an attempt to pull me clear of the vehicle's door. He wanted to open it. Get to Abby.

"No! You asshole. Let me go!" I squirmed and fought, eventually slapping him across the face with my right hand. Hard. Really fucking hard.

He stumbled back, a look of pure shock on his face. Dominique was in the driver's seat, engine running, yelling at me to *get in.* I hurried, climbed into the passenger seat, and slammed the door closed. I hit the locks immediately, uncaring that the bottom of my dress was stuck in the doorframe, probably hanging like a curtain outside the SUV. I'd fix it when we came to a stoplight. Time to get the hell out of here.

"Go! I'm in. Go!"

Dominique hit the gas, and the SUV's tires squealed on the pavement like we were fleeing the hounds of hell. That's what it felt like. If Tane hadn't been there with his friends to stop the reporters? The paparazzi? The aggressive, intrusive jerks who would do anything to get a picture they could sell? We wouldn't have made it.

Dominique didn't stop the SUV until we were three blocks away, running several stop signs and one bright red stoplight to get us as far away as possible, as quickly as she could. She finally stopped so I could open the door and pull the rest of my ridiculous dress inside. Once we were sure we weren't being followed, she pulled off and wove her way through a residential neighborhood. No doubt the paparazzi would try to pick up our trail as we made our way back to the Gregg mansion. No sense taking the main roads to get there. No one famous enough to run from the paparazzi had forgotten what happened to Princess Diana all those years ago. No one with any sense, anyway. I didn't want to be run off the road and die in a car accident because some jerk wanted a picture.

Leaning back in the seat, I closed my eyes and thought about Tane. The way he kissed. The way he smelled. The way he'd gone down on one knee on the stairs and asked me to dance with him. I was so preoccupied it took me a full ten minutes to notice that my great-grandmother's locket was gone. My wrist was bare. That jerk who'd grabbed me must have broken the clasp.

No. No. No. I should have listened to Dominique and left it at home. But no. I never went anywhere without it. Never. Now it was gone.

Shaking, I wrapped my hand around my wrist and fought back tears. I'd left Tane behind. I'd lost my locket. And for what?

For the teenager in the back seat with eyes too old for

her young face. I'd been working with her for three years as her private tutor, using my teaching degree to keep her up to speed with other teenagers her age as she traveled the world and focused on her *career*. What child had a career before eighteen? The young lady was unique. Talented. Stubborn. Smart. And she had wiggled her way into my heart. I loved her like a little sister. I knew she had a heart as fragile as glass. I knew what it was to lose my parents. Face the world alone. Abby, for all her bravado, cried the entire hour it took us to drive back to the ten-acre complex she called home. I cried with her.

5

ane, *Four hours later*

I HELD my mate's golden locket in one hand and her invitation to the ball in the other. Katinka Friðfinnsdóttir, I had discovered, was traveling on another continent with her fiancé, a man named David. She had long blonde hair, blue eyes, and was *not* the woman I had fucked last night. She was not my mate.

Worse, no one named Elena was on the guest list.

Nor was there an Abby, the younger female my mate had been so worried about.

The male seated on the opposite side of the table stared at me like I was a monster.

He hadn't seen a beast yet, but if he refused to answer me again, he would. Soon. "Tell me human, why did you attack the women?"

"I didn't attack them," he denied

My beast growled, impatient. It was four o'clock in the morning. I would not rest until I had answers.

"The red handprint on your face would suggest otherwise."

The man sighed and held up both hands, palms out. "Look, man, I'm just trying to make a living. If I'd gotten a picture of the girl here, last night, I could pay my rent for a year, all right. I would never hurt her, but I gotta eat. You feel me?"

"No." I did not *feel* anything but the need to tear this man's head from his shoulders. He'd placed his hands on my mate. Hurt her. Torn the golden chain from her wrist. She had been threatened enough to slap him. That both pleased me and made me rage at the same time.

I should have been there to stop this idiot. At the same time I was oddly proud that my mate had managed to defeat him herself.

"Let me talk to him, please?" Barhe's mate, Quinn, had been watching and listening when the Prillon guards hauled the man in. They'd had to track him to his apartment, drag him from his home, and bring him to me. I'd wanted to go after him myself, but Bahre had wisely pointed out that in my current state there was a high probability I would have simply killed him for touching Elena.

That remained a possibility.

Unable to speak around the beast's rumble in my chest, I stepped aside and gestured for the Lady Quinn to take the seat opposite my prisoner. That's what he was, my prisoner. At my mercy.

Quinn looked up at me from where she was seated at

the table. "Tane, do you mind? You're scaring the crap out of him."

"Good." I wanted him scared. Repentant. Terrified. "He laid his hands on a female. He doesn't deserve to survive the night."

"Go. Stand over there." Quinn pointed to the far wall where Bahre stood guarding his mate. I moved to stand next to him and wait.

Clearing her throat, Quinn looked at my prisoner and smiled at him. "I think we got off on the wrong foot."

"Those brutes dragged me out of bed."

"I know. I'm sorry about that."

"I want a lawyer."

"We aren't the police, Mr. Kroger. We just need some information about tonight."

The man was wearing a pair of fuzzy pants, no shirt, and his feet were bare. "What do you want to know?"

"Who was the young lady you tried to photograph tonight?"

He looked shocked. "You don't know? What? You live in a cave?" He leaned back in the chair with a smug smirk on his face and crossed his arms over his chest.

"No. But I did not see her. You did. Who was she?"

"Listen, sweetheart, I know who she is. I also know who you are. You let me go now and I won't sue you and your alien husband for every goddamn dime you've got. Okay?" The man tilted his head, a cruel twist to his lips as he looked at Quinn. Bahre tensed beside me. I wanted to nudge him and tell him to control himself. Be calm. Rational.

Not so fucking easy when this man was threatening *his* mate.

Quinn's eyes narrowed and I saw the fire within, knew that passion was one of the reasons Bahre was so in love with her. "Listen, you little asshole, you are going to tell me who she is, right now, or I'm going to let these aliens take you back to their spaceship, torture you, experiment on you, and scatter the tiny pieces of your bloody, broken body on the moon. No one will ever know you were here, and no one will ever find your body. You feel me?"

His smile faded and his skin turned a pasty gray. "Okay. Okay. Jesus. It's not like it's a big secret. Abigail Gregg. You know, the fucking heiress? Daddy's little darling?"

Quinn leaned forward. "George Gregg's daughter?"

"That's the one."

"And the two women with her?"

The man shrugged. "I don't know. I think one of them was her manager or something. I don't know who the other one was, the one that slapped me. Got a mean right hand, I'll tell you that. But that girl's got an entourage, you know? Everyone wants to be wherever she is. She's worth billions."

"She's eighteen."

"So? She's legal. She's old enough to marry one of these aliens. You know how much a picture of her with one of these guys would be worth?" He lifted his hand, fingers curled, thumb pointing in my direction. "And oh fuck, would her daddy be furious. Shit would hit the fan. He hates them fucking aliens." He glanced at Bahre over his shoulder. "No offense."

Bahre didn't bother to respond. I didn't dare. The more he spoke, the more I fantasized about killing him.

Quinn stood and walked to us. "Tell the Prillons to

take him home and leave him. We don't need him anymore."

Bahre nodded and left us to do as his mate requested. Seconds later two Prillon warriors in black escorted the filthy human from the room.

I was confused. "You released him? He did not tell us about my mate."

"No. But now we know how to find her."

"You are sure, my lady? I cannot lose her."

She looked at me with concern in her eyes. "I'm sure. Trust me. We find Abigail Gregg; we'll find your mate."

Bahre returned to her side and wrapped his arm around her waist, pulled her close. She melted against him as I imagined Elena would give herself to me. "Experiments? Scatter tiny pieces on the moon?" He chuckled and I found myself grinning along with him. "You know we don't do that, love. No spaceships in orbit around Earth, either."

"I know that, but clearly he did not." Quinn was smiling now too.

Bahre leaned down and kissed her quickly on the lips. "You are delightful, mate."

She shrugged. "What I am is ruthless. We need to find Elena. Abigail Gregg is the key. George Gregg owns a large building in the city, and I'm pretty sure Abigail has a streaming studio there."

"Let's go." I didn't want to waste another moment. I had been away from my mate for too long already.

Quinn shook her head. "It's the weekend. The offices will be closed."

"What about his home? Surely his daughter will be there."

"Sure. Great. Guys like him will probably have a dozen armed guards toting machine guns, a dozen really mean dogs, and security cameras everywhere. And you heard that guy. He wasn't wrong. It's well-known that George Gregg hates the Coalition, hates the Interstellar Brides Program, hates all of it. He has his people out digging up dirt all the time. He's even done a couple of not very nice articles on me and Bahre."

"He has?" Why had I never heard of this human male before? He was clearly a threat to us.

"We have to be discreet. Go to his office. Poke around a bit. See what we can find out. I did a search on Katinka. She works for Gregg Media, has a private office in the building. I'm guessing that's how Elena got her hands on the invitation."

"I do not want to wait." My beast paced inside me. Raged. My words were beyond an understatement.

"I'm sorry, Tane. We have to. No one will be there until Monday morning."

"Fuck."

Bahre's large hand clamped down on my shoulder. "You found her, brother. Your mate. She is here, on Earth. She is alive. She is beautiful. She didn't run from your touch. Be calm. We will find her."

Be calm. Was he fucking serious? I looked down at the locket in my hand. I had opened the golden oval. Discovered a photograph inside. "Look at this. Elena was wearing it tonight." I placed the locket in Quinn's palm and waited as she inspected the locket.

"Hmm." Quinn turned it over and squinted to read the faded engraving. "John fifteen thirteen."

I held my tongue as she opened the device and looked at the image of a young man inside. "Wow."

"Is that John? Why would my mate be carrying the image of a man if he were not important to her?" I was terrified of the question, but I had to know.

Quinn gently closed the locket and handed it back to me. "That's an antique, Tane. Looks like it's at least eighty, maybe a hundred years old. The picture inside is probably one of her ancestors, maybe a grandfather or great-grandfather. Looks like he was a soldier. If I had to guess, I'd say World War I. So, a hundred years old, at least?"

"An ancestor. And his name was John? Could that not aid us in our search?" I nearly crumbled with relief. I did not wish to battle another male for my mate's heart. Worse, if she loved this other human, I would be forced to walk away and accept my fate. My beast had chosen Elena and would choose no other. If we could not be with Elena, we would face the executioner's blade on Atlan, die an honorable death.

Quinn shook her head. "No, that's John 15:13. It's a Bible verse."

Ah. Human religion. I was about to ask what this verse meant, but Quinn already had her cell phone in her hands and was doing a search for the information. She read aloud, "John 15:13. 'Greater love hath no man than this: that a man lay down his life for his friends.'"

I understood at once. "This human died in battle protecting his family, his people. He died a warrior's death."

Quinn shrugged. "Maybe. I don't know. You'll have to ask her about it when you find her. But clearly it was important to her. She'll be very happy to have it returned."

Excellent. I would find my mate, give her this precious locket, and place my mating cuffs around her wrists. She would not escape again.

———

ELENA

WHY WAS the proverbial lord of the manor summoning me to his office at this ungodly hour? It was a Sunday. It was way past my bedtime. And he'd only been back from his trip to Asia for a few hours. Didn't the man ever sleep?

Not that Mr. Gregg had ever cared about anyone's schedule but his own.

I followed the butler as he led the way to Mr. Gregg's office. I was wearing a matching set of black satin pajama shirt and matching shorts, fuzzy slippers, and a robe that tied at my waist with a hem that fell just past my knees. I didn't bother with my hair or makeup. If he wanted me dressed and put together, he could damn well talk to me during the day, not the wee hours of the morning.

Not that I'd been sleeping. I'd barely slept the last two nights. All I could do was toss and turn and think about Tane.

The butler knocked on Mr. Gregg's door. "Sir? Miss Garcia to see you, sir."

"Send her in."

The butler opened the door and held it for me with a

nod of his head. I stepped inside to find the weasel I'd slapped yesterday looking smug on his way out.

"What are you doing here?"

"Miss." He smirked at me and walked past.

"Where's my locket?" He was the one who had grabbed me, broken the chain. It was his fault I'd lost it. He had to have seen it lying there in the parking lot.

"Ask your psycho alien boyfriend." The man of the broken nose and scarred lip shouted the words over his shoulder as he headed toward the front of the house. The butler hurried to follow him. I stared, gaping. *Psycho alien boyfriend?* What the hell was this guy ranting about? And why had he been here? He didn't get any pictures of Abby. I'd made sure of that when I slammed the car door in his face.

The heavy wooden door of Mr. Gregg's office swung closed on its own, settling into place with a soft *click*. I was now trapped inside the room with my boss.

Lovely.

Turning around slowly, I faced Mr. Gregg, who was standing in front of his desk, one hip propped on the corner so he appeared to be half-seated. He liked to talk to me when he was standing. I had figured out a long time ago that he didn't want me to be looking down at him when he was ordering me around.

This was not the first time I'd been standing in front of George Gregg's desk wondering what transgression I'd committed or what demand he would make of me. It was, however, the first time he'd had the large television screen along the wall turned on.

I froze.

Shit.

That was me, standing at the top of the stairs, looking like an honest-to-God princess. Dominique had been correct. The dress was stunning. I looked amazing. Too gorgeous to be real. Tane's back had been to the camera, but it was obvious he was on bended knee, kneeling before me just like a prince in a fairy tale. I knew he'd been asking me to dance.

A dance. A kiss. And so much more. So much.

"Was she there, Elena? Was. She. There? And don't lie to me."

6

I CAREFULLY CONSIDERED my answer as I studied Tane's broad shoulders and dark hair on the frozen screen. Mr. Gregg had paused the video, and I noticed, oddly, that television-me was nearly half as tall as the real me standing here now. George Gregg did not purchase anything but the biggest and best of everything. I didn't know they even made screens this big.

"Yes, sir." I had no doubt the scum paparazzi who had just left had told Mr. Gregg everything. "She thought it would be good for her career, get her extra publicity, but decided against going through with her plans once we had encountered the aliens." We both knew who *she* referred to. His daughter. Abigail. I turned from the screen to face him and lied. Flat-out lied. "Abigail knows how you feel about the Coalition. She might parade her boyfriends in front of you to get a reaction, but she knows better now. She would not dare involve one of the alien males. She realized that any one of them would be beyond her ability to control. She is not willing to take that risk. Your daughter is highly intelligent and calculating, sir. Dominique and I helped her escape before anyone realized she was there."

I looked back over my shoulder at the door. "Well, almost anyone. And he didn't get any pictures of Abigail. I made sure of that."

"Yes." Mr. Gregg actually grinned at me like I was a co-conspirator. "He showed me the handprint you left on his face. Nicely done, Elena. But my daughter should not have been there at all."

"Your daughter has a very strong will. But Abigail assessed the situation and decided we should leave at once. She is very astute, sir, and careful not to take risks with her career." I prattled on about Abby in order to please him. He liked to think his daughter was a chip off the old block. The apple that had not fallen far from the tree. He didn't want Abby to be an emotional young woman with genuine compassion or feelings. It was so much easier for him to believe she was ruthless, ambitious, and cold. Like him.

He stared into my eyes for long moments, looking for weakness. I stared back, unmoved. We'd played this game before.

Silence stretched for close to a minute before he raised his hand and gestured toward the screen. He held a remote control. "Shall I fast-forward to the dance? To the dazed look on your face as that alien beast put his filthy, lying hands all over you?"

"No, sir. I remember what happened. I don't need to watch it again." Oh, but I did. I was going straight to my room to scour the Internet for this exact video clip. I wanted to watch it again. Maybe a thousand times. It would be like reliving a dream.

"If my daughter had decided to leave this godforsaken circus, why were you still there?"

I shrugged. "I've never met an alien. I was curious."

"You left the room with him. What happened?"

"Nothing." Sheesh, who did this guy think he was? My father? I knew he didn't care about me as a person. He only cared about my connection to him, to his daughter, to his media empire. "He asked me for another dance. I declined." I held up my hands, wrists bare to emphasize my point. "You know how those aliens work. See? No mating cuffs."

"He didn't insist you were his mate?"

"No. If he had, do you think he would have let me out of his sight?"

"Hmmm. They are obsessive once they have claimed a woman." He pushed a button on the remote, and the images of me and Tane came to life. Him, leading me down the stairs. Our dance. God, I could literally feel his arms around me, feel the heat of him. Hear his voice. Feel his cock spreading me open, filling me to the brink of pain, pushing me over it into pleasure. The way he smelled. The lingering sweetness of his lips on my neck. Suckling at my breast. The soft strands of his hair sliding though my fingers.

I was wet and needy and missing Tane so badly I almost forgot where I was. Almost.

"Do you see the way that monster is looking at you?"

I studied Tane's face on the screen and nearly forgot to breathe. He was looking into my face like he was totally, madly in love with me. Like there was no other woman in the room. Was he that talented an actor? Or had I missed something very, very important?

But no. He hadn't said anything about mating cuffs. Or called me his mate. Had he?

I tried to remember every moment I'd spent with Tane, replay every word spoken, but Mr. Gregg interrupted.

"I know how men think. Alien. Human. Makes no difference. He wants to fuck you. He will come for you. Track you down."

"Sir?" I had no idea what to say to that or what Mr. Gregg wanted from me.

"I want you to let him find you, Elena. Invite him into the house. Flirt with him. Make him comfortable."

"Excuse me?" Had he been snorting crazy powder? This was so not like him.

"Keep your friends close and your enemies closer, Elena. This is the opportunity I've been waiting for. In fact, I'm going to make sure he finds you."

"What? Why?"

"That is not your concern. You will be gracious. Invite him into the house. Keep him here as long as possible. Do you understand?"

"I—yes." My heart was racing with excitement at the thought of seeing Tane again even as my skin went cold with dread.

Mr. Gregg turned off the video, and the screen went black. Cold. Dark. "You will be well-dressed and waiting in the second-floor conference room by nine tomorrow morning. Do I make myself clear?"

"Yes." Gregg Media Building. Second floor. Nine a.m. "Got it. Nine o'clock."

Apparently satisfied, he waved his hand at me in a dismissive gesture I knew meant I could return to my room.

I left before he could change his mind, the scuffling sound of my slippers on the cool marble floor eerie in the dark hallway. *Whoosh. Whoosh. Whoosh.*

I didn't bother to pick up my feet; they were lead weights anchoring me to this new hell, a hell where I was expected to help destroy the most perfect man I'd ever met.

Abby's father had something terrible planned for Tane. For the other Atlans. And he demanded I play along.

As thrilled as I was at the idea of seeing Tane again, I was worried too. I would do everything Mr. Gregg instructed. Invite Tane in. Be kind and courteous.

And take the first opportunity to warn him that something evil was afoot.

Knowing Mr. Gregg's hatred for the Coalition and all the aliens from the Coalition worlds, Mr. Gregg's plan would be cruel. Dangerous. Hurtful. Not just to Tane but to his friends.

And what was that paparazzi jerk doing here? Why had he called Tane a *serial killer alien*? What was that supposed to mean? Because if they expected me to believe Tane was going around murdering people, they had lost their minds. No way. No. Just no.

So I would play along. If this charade was the only

way to protect Tane and figure out what Mr. Gregg had planned, I didn't have a choice.

————

TANE, Gregg Media Building

"RIGHT THIS WAY, Mr.—umm—Mr. Warlord, sir." The young man leading the way through the building was thin, barely more than a child, and stuttering over nearly every word he spoke.

"I need to speak to Dominique Dimont, Miss Gregg's publicist. I know she has an office in the building." I knew because we'd spent the last twenty-four hours learning everything we could about Abigail Gregg, Dominique Dimont, and looking—without luck—for Elena.

"Yes, of course, sir. We've been expecting you." He nodded furiously, his chin bobbing up and down like a robotic arm in a factory. "In fact, Mr. Gregg sent me to the lobby first thing this morning to wait for your arrival."

Either Elena didn't exist, or she wasn't on the Gregg company payroll. Which meant she knew Abby personally. I'd dedicated hours to pouring over the young lady's social media feeds. Thousands of photographs. Not one included Elena.

Not one.

I was ready to kill someone if I had to, in order to find her. Hopefully that wouldn't be necessary. Dominique had been easy to find. And she knew Elena, very well. They had been at the ball together. She would tell me where I could find my mate. She must. The beast was clawing at my insides with new levels of fury. He would find her if I did not. Most likely leave a pile of bodies and total destruction every step of the way.

The young assistant led me to an elevator. Reluctantly I followed him inside and waited for the doors to slide closed.

"Conference room on the second floor. Yes, sir."

"Fine." I hated closed spaces. The air was too hot, the walls too close. I narrowed my eyes as the floor lurched beneath my feet. I should have brought backup. Half a dozen warlords, at least. But I'd been warned against it, by Quinn. She had promised me that even one beast showing up at her work might scare my mate. If I appeared with a small army, she might be terrified. Or worse, run.

With a *ding*, the doors slid open, and the man scuttled ahead of me like his back was on fire. "Right this way. Follow me."

The conference room was clearly labeled with a plaque next to the door. The walls were mostly glass, covered from within by shades that had been closed to provide privacy to the room's occupants.

Not waiting for an invitation, I opened the door and glanced inside.

Dominique sat at the head of the table looking serene and confident. On her left was Elena in a dark blue suit and gray blouse. Her hair was pulled up in a tight knot at the back of her head, and her skin looked pale.

"Warlord Tane. Please, come in." Dominique invited me in, and I moved into the room, closing the door behind me.

"Elena, my lady. You disappeared."

"I'm sorry. Extenuating circumstances."

My heart became a bit lighter at her words. Perhaps she had not wanted to leave me. Perhaps she would find me worthy, choose to be my mate, accept my mating cuffs and my devotion.

If so, why was she sitting stiff and unyielding in the chair as far away from the door as possible? Why was she not already in my arms, her head nestled against my chest, her body molded to mine?

"We had to get Abby out of there, Tane. Sorry about that. It was kind of an emergency." Dominique leaned back in her chair and was tapping the end of a pen on the long meeting table.

Elena tore her gaze from mine and turned to look at Dominique. "Did you know he would be here?"

Dominique shook her head. "No. He told me to be here but didn't tell me why. Just like you."

Elena looked up at me, her dark eyes full of fear. Hurt. "You shouldn't be here, Tane. You should go. Now." She looked past me as if she could see through the door. "Hurry. I'll—"

The door swung open, and an older human male joined us. "You'll what, my dear?" The man held out his hand to me in the human way. He was older, perhaps sixty, with graying hair and an expensive suit. He carried an air of command, a man used to being obeyed without question.

He met my gaze, looking up at me with narrowed eyes. "George Gregg. Pleasure to meet the man who helped get my daughter out of trouble. A pleasure."

That was not what I had been expecting, but I was not

displeased. Relaxing a fraction, I accepted the man's handshake. Elena and Dominique both stood as I turned to face them. "Elena, I need to speak with you."

"Of course you do." George's hand pounded on the back of my shoulder as if we were old friends. We were not. I turned to look down on him, my beast's displeasure changing the shape of my face. George stepped back with a frown that quickly morphed into a forced smile. "Of course you need to speak to our Elena. After what happened at the ball, I knew you would want to see her again."

"I do. I would speak to her, in private."

"Of course. Of course." He glanced from me to Elena, and a peculiar look passed between them.

Something strange was happening here. My instincts were raging at me that Elena was in danger, but from what? This weak human male?

7

GEORGE STEPPED AWAY from me and walked slowly around the table. As he did so, Elena's body grew stiffer, her face drawn as if she were worried. About what? Me? Did she truly not wish to be alone with me? Had I frightened her? Moved too quickly at the ball? She had found pleasure in my arms, but she seemed confused. Unsure.

I focused on my senses and drew her scent deeply into my body. Processed what I could of her emotional state from the chemicals on her skin.

She was nervous. Angry. Afraid. Of what? Of me?

Fuck. What had I done?

"I've had a car brought around for you. It will take you both to my estate, Warlord. You'll have privacy there. I assure you. I hire only the best, private security, former Special Forces. The property is ten acres, and Elena has her own suite of rooms. You'll be comfortable there and protected from prying eyes."

Was this man serious? Did he truly believe I would hand over the protection of my mate to a bunch of humans? I did not know the term *Special Forces*, but I assumed he referred to the human military. I had experience with such fighters. Humans now made up a large number of the ReCon Units in the Coalition Fleet. Units like the one that had found me in that Hive detention cell and set me free. Humans were good fighters. Quiet. Efficient. Brutal when they had to be. But they were not Atlan warlords.

Even before the Hive had modified my body, my beast could take a hundred bullets from their puny human weapons and still tear a dozen human guards into pieces. With the Hive integrations? I did not know what I was capable of. I'd never tested my limits. Part of me did not want to know what new abilities the Hive had given me. I was acutely aware of my heightened sense of taste. Touch. Smell. Of the continual buzzing of Hive communications inside my mind. I did not want to be grateful for any part of the torture I'd endured. And yet I could still taste Elena on my tongue, smell her feminine scent from across the room.

"Is this what you wish, Elena?"

Dominique looked from me to Elena like she wanted to say something but remained silent.

"Yes. I need to speak to you too."

George moved behind Elena and steered her in my direction. Elena shifted toward me quickly, just fast enough to avoid contact with the other man. A fact I was grateful for. George Gregg might be acting as if he were

Elena's father, but I knew he was not. He was a man whose gaze lingered on Dominique's breasts, on Elena's lips. If he had touched my mate in her current state—nervous, anxious, and afraid—my beast would have demanded to be free, to protect our female, our mate.

MINE.

The word was growled into my mind, my beast making his intentions clear. He wanted Elena. Needed her. Would die to protect her.

My mate came to a stop before me and looked up into my face. She was close now, close enough to keep her safe. My beast relaxed as I held out my hand to Elena, as I'd done on the stairs at the ball. Slowly she placed her hand in mine. Desperate to reassure her, I leaned down and pressed my kiss to her slender wrist. "My lady. Thank you for your trust. You will come to no harm with me."

George cleared his throat. "I'm sure Elena would feel more comfortable at home, in familiar surroundings. I have a car downstairs, waiting to take you home."

"I have my own transportation." I did, too. A vehicle with bulletproof glass and two members of Bahre's security team waiting to escort me and my mate. Assuming she agreed to come with me.

"You won't need it, my boy. Isn't that right, Elena? Wouldn't you feel more comfortable at home?"

"I—" Elena looked at me and I could not tolerate the doubt I saw in her gaze.

"Very well. Elena's comfort comes first." Perhaps the elder was correct. Elena would feel safe and secure in her own home, surrounded by familiar things. She would believe the human guards could protect her if I tried to attack her. The thought was beyond ludicrous, even my beast scoffed at the very thought that we would harm our mate, but Elena was human, with a human mind and human expectations. If anything, Quinn had pounded that fact into our thick Atlan skulls the last few weeks.

I made quick use of my human cell phone and sent a message to my team to go back to Bahre's home and wait for my call.

"Excellent." George walked to the door and swung it wide, calling out for the same young man who had brought me up in the elevator. When he appeared, George instructed him to take us to the front of the building where a car was waiting.

Elena's hand trembled in mine, and she pulled away from my touch once we were in the elevator. She glanced nervously around, her gaze flitting from the control panel to the camera mounted in the corner.

Was she afraid someone would see her showing me affection? Accepting my touch?

My beast screamed in agony. This could not be happening. Surely the gods would not be this cruel. Had I not suffered enough? Now I would be forced to endure rejection from my mate?

I did not attempt to touch her again until we were seated in the large vehicle. The driver closed the door, and we were alone in the back of a stretch SUV with seats large enough to hold several Atlans and their mates without an issue.

Unable to bear it another moment, I reached across to the opposite seat and lifted Elena from the leather. Leaning back, I placed her in my lap, where she belonged.

"Tane, I don't think this is a good idea."

"We need to talk, and I cannot go another moment without touching you."

As if my words broke through whatever wall she had erected, she sighed and relaxed against my chest. I wrapped my arms around her to support her back, and she rested her cheek over my heart. We sat in silence for long moments. I hoped she would confide in me, tell what was troubling her. When she did not offer any information, I tried again.

"Elena, when we were together at the ball—"

"Shhh!" Her fingertip came to settle on my lips. "Shhh. Not here."

"Elena, I will not—"

"Tane!" She nearly shouted my name, moving her hand from in front of my mouth to the side of my face, then slid her fingers into my hair. The sensation brought back memories, and my cock hardened where it pressed to her plump, round, perfect ass. When she tugged my head down to one side, closer to her, I did not resist. I had neither the desire nor the will to resist this woman.

Her lips teased my ear with the lightest touch as she murmured, "Can you hear me? Squeeze me if you can understand what I'm saying."

I squeezed her ass, happy to do so. Her voice was not even a whisper, more like a hint of sound. Without my integrations, I would not be able to make out her words above the noise of the vehicle's tires on the road, the wind outside. The privacy screen was up and locked in place, but I could still hear the music our driver was listening to, as well as his off-key, sing-along voice.

Her lips pressed to my ear in a kiss, and my beast, already alarmed, seemed to snap to attention.

"We can't talk here. Don't say anything. It's not safe."

Not safe?

The change started at once, and I had no control over the beast. None. Our mate was in danger, she'd been acting strangely since the moment we saw her, and now she admitted to me that she was in danger?

"No." My beast's voice was much deeper, harsher. I grew in stature until I had to duck my head against the vehicle's ceiling, stretch my legs out in front of me until they reached the other seat. Even then I had to bend my knees to make them fit. Through it all I held my mate on my lap, both unwilling and unable to let her go.

Elena had gone still in my arms. Now that the change was complete, she leaned back, pressing against the arm I had placed behind her torso, and looked up into the beast's face.

"Well, you must be the beast?"

"Yes." The beast leaned in close and took a deep breath, enjoying the sweet scent of her skin for the first time. "Mine."

"I told you not to say anything."

The beast snorted in disgust. "Mine. Protect. Safe." Nothing in this vehicle frightened him. Nothing on this Earth, for that matter. Nothing but losing her.

"You only speak in one-word sentences? Tane, are you still in there?" She looked deeply into the beast's eyes, completely unafraid. My fierce female. "You guys fight like this, right? So you know what's going on? You understand everything? Your brain still works?"

My beast smiled at our adorable mate. Of course he understood everything. He was a warlord, a commander, a veteran of many battles. He knew when the vehicle's tires hit a rock, when an insect died, its liquid insides smashed against the windshield. He knew how many other cars were on the road, their size, how fast they were going. He knew the exact timing of Elena's heartbeat and the scent of her shampoo. He knew she'd put that horrible-smelling paint on her toenails this morning; the tart odor lingered on her feet, teased him from within her high-heeled shoes.

He wondered what color she'd chosen. Red? Blue? He wanted to kiss her toes and find out.

He wanted to kiss her everywhere.

So did I.

My cock, already hard, swelled to painful proportions. Elena wiggled in my lap, the movement not at all helpful. "Oh dear. We can't do that, beast. Not in here."

"Not safe."

She seemed to wilt in relief. "Exactly."

She had not said she did not want to fuck the beast. Nor was she acting as if she was afraid of him. Both things that pleased us greatly. But above all, the beast reveled in the scent of her arousal, her need. The scent of her wet pussy made my chest rumble. She would welcome the beast into her body, take his cock, wear the mating cuffs I had stashed in my satchel. We would claim her. Today.

"Mine."

"You already said that."

"Kiss." I lowered my lips to her cheek, her nose, the corner of her mouth. She turned into me and offered her mouth. I took her lips with a hunger I had never known before. Urgent. Desperate. I needed this female. She was life. Blood. My heartbeat.

"God, you're dangerous." She tore her lips from mine and scrambled away from me to curl up in a seat as far from me as possible. "I told you, we can't do that here."

"Protect you. Safe."

She shook her head. "No, Tane. Not from this. Trust me. We have to wait."

I did not like her words, but I sat back, content to please her. For now. Her pussy was wetter after the kiss, her feminine scent stronger. Her skin was heated, the beast able to track her body's preparation for sex. For mating. Human hormones were raging through her blood, and I could smell each one of them. They called to the beast the way honey attracted the bee. I would not be able to resist her. Not today. Not ever. She would own me, body and soul, and I was prepared to give myself to her, to kneel before her, to die protecting her. Elena. I would surrender to no other, obey no other, serve no other.

Only her. My mate.

Mine.

The beast wanted to shout it to the world, but we had already spoken our claim too many times. Saying it again would only upset our delicate female. So I remained silent, content to study her in this new clothing. Her ball gown had been magnificent, true. But I sensed this was her day-to-day attire, the manner in which she preferred to dress.

I approved. Of course, she could be wearing a sack or nothing at all and I would be equally content. But her clothing was similar to that worn by Bahre's mate, Quinn. What she had called professional business attire. Elene wore a skirt that stopped right at her knees, a blouse tucked inside a matching dark blue jacket. She looked prim and proper and like she had too many clothes on.

"Beautiful."

My deep voice startled her, and she jumped in her seat. She truly was nervous. "Thank you, Beast. You're not so bad yourself." She took a moment to inspect my beast, and we sat still, waiting for her judgment. "I thought you'd be big and hairy or something. You don't look that different, really. Just bigger."

Fuck yes, I was bigger. Stronger. With my Hive integrations, I was nearly indestructible. My cock was bigger as well. Eager to fill her. Make her mine—ours—forever.

"It takes a while to get to the Gregg estate. Might as well get comfortable."

I looked out the window, impatient to be out of this vehicle and alone with my mate so she could tell me what was going on. And so I could fuck her senseless. And not necessarily in that order.

She looked at her cell phone, probably to avoid the intense, I-want-to-fuck-you look I knew my beast was giving her. I didn't try to scold him or hold him back. I was in full agreement. Elena was soft and curved and mine. So fucking mine.

She cleared her throat. "Sheesh. Another forty-five minutes. And that's if we don't hit traffic."

My beast grumbled his frustration with that answer. "Too long." I dropped my hand to my lap and stroked my hard cock through the pants I wore.

"Stop that." She blushed but she didn't look away. "Put that thing away before you get us both in trouble."

"Want me."

She stared directly into the beast's eyes. "Yes. But not here. Behave."

My mate had said yes. That was all I needed to hear. Despite being called a beast, I was not an animal. I could wait to fuck her. Kiss her. Shove that blue skirt up over her round ass and feast on her sweet pussy. I would not be rushed, not this time. She would scream my name. She would beg for more. Beg me to stop. Beg for my cock. My tongue. My hands.

She would beg for release. She would demand and I would provide. She was mine.

I feasted my eyes on her feminine form the rest of the journey. Drew her scent deep into my lungs and branded her into my memory. Every cell in my body would recognize her.

By the time we pulled through a set of elaborate gates, I was nearly out of patience. The security guard cleared the driver, and we moved on to a long drive that wound through thick foliage and trees toward a massive home even bigger than the one Bahre had acquired for his mate.

I opened the door the moment the vehicle rolled to a stop. Took a deep breath. Scanned the area.

Swamp. Trees. I could distinguish the presence of eight different dogs as well as at least a dozen men. They were all armed with human guns, the distinct tang of metal and gun oil coming from multiple directions.

An older gentleman in a black suit hurried to greet us as I assisted Elena from the vehicle. "Welcome, Warlord Tane. We have been expecting you. I have prepared the guest suit. I hope you will find the accommodations suitable."

Hand firmly at the base of Elena's spine, I straightened to my full height. The man took a step back.

So he wasn't as stupid as he looked.

Elena cleared her throat. "Tane, this is Mr. Gregg's butler, Tony. He's been with Mr. Gregg for more than twenty years."

"Good." I nodded at the man and rubbed my palm up and down Elena's lower back. I had gotten her message. Loyal to George. Not safe. Got it.

Elena looked from me to Tony. "Shall we go inside before we melt?"

"Of course, of course." Tony hurried to the door and led us into a marbled space with ascending staircases wrapped around either side of a large circular rotunda. A chandelier hung over our heads that was three times the size of those I'd seen at the ball. Marble statues of sea creatures as well as human nudes were placed strategically around the area. Paintings in gilded frames were spaced along the walls above the stairs in exactly equal measure.

Mr. Gregg had money, and he wanted people to know he had money.

Elena walked past all of it completely unimpressed, as if she'd seen it a thousand times. Perhaps she had.

Why did she live here? What hold did the master of this house have over my mate?

"This way, sir."

Tony the Butler led the way past several long corridors, around corners, up two flights of stairs, down another hall, and stopped in front of a large, closed door. "Here we are, Mr. Warlord, sir. This suite has been prepared especially for you. Should you need anything,

anything at all, press the intercom button, and I will answer at once."

Elena moved between Tony and the door, blocking the entrance. "Thanks, Tony. I've got it from here."

Tony looked offended, his chest puffed out and a frown across his brow, but he dipped his chin in acceptance and left.

Elena opened the door, and I followed her inside. The moment it closed, I pressed her back to the door and leaned down to kiss her.

I was met with her small finger once more pressed to my lips and slight shake of her head.

"Not yet," she whispered.

Her gaze darted to the side, and she slipped out beneath my arm and walked deeper into the room. I could not complain about the suite. Giant bed. Shimmering sheets. Light shining in the windows, and heavy wooden furniture situated around the room for ease of use. A desk. Two chairs. A television and a sofa with a small table. The room was painted in shades of green and gold that reminded me of the leaves on Earth's trees. The space was warm and comfortable.

Why was Elena pacing? Peeking behind the plants? The paintings?

She leaned forward, her nose nearly touching the wall as she inspected what I assumed was a fire monitor of some type.

"Elena?"

"Shhh." Turning around, she looked at the shelves of the small bookcase. She jumped. Jumped again. "Damn it, I'm too short."

She also could not get very high off the floor, but I would not insult her by pointing this out.

Instead I walked to where she stood, placed my hands around her waist, and lifted her until her head was level with the top shelf. "Good?"

"Yes." She reached for something, placed it in her hand, and looked down at me. "There are some really good books on the top shelf. I grabbed one I think you'll enjoy. You can put me down now."

I settled her on her feet, taking the opportunity to slide her small body along mine. My cock remained hard. I was beginning to suspect it would be a permanent condition with my female near.

Instead of pushing me away, she grabbed my hand and pulled me toward the far end of the room. With a calm, clear voice she finally spoke up. "Come on, Tane. You haven't seen the bathroom yet. Wait until you see the size of the tub. Even a beast can soak in it."

I followed her inside the bathing room, and she immediately twisted the handles on the bathtub. The loud roar of water filled the room. She stepped back, dropped something on the hard tile floor, and crushed it beneath her shoe without looking down.

Bending down after the fact, she picked up the remains of the object before pulling me close. She reached for my hand. Turning my palm up, she placed the small item in the center. "These are everywhere. You can't say anything or do anything he can use against you. He hates the Coalition. He's looking for ammunition. Don't give him anything he can use."

8

TANE SCOWLED and studied the high-tech bug I'd just dropped into his palm. When he was a beast, his expressions were much more difficult to read. Was he angry? Shocked? Upset? Nervous? Scared?

No. The last two were me. I was shaking so badly I didn't know how much longer I could stand in these heels.

He lifted the small object to eye level, and I watched, fascinated, as something that looked like silver computer code, streaks of electricity, moved behind his eyes.

I knew, intellectually, that Tane was from The Colony. I'd read that the men—aliens—who lived there had been captured by the evil Hive, the enemy of the entire Coalition and the reason for their deal with Earth, and turned into cyborgs. But it hadn't seemed real to me until now.

What else did he have hidden under those clothes? Under his skin? Inside his body? We'd had sex with our clothes on. I hadn't seen anything, not his chest or his ass or even his cock. Did he have metal body parts? Bits that lit up like Christmas lights? What did it mean to be a cyborg? His eyes had looked completely normal every time I stared into them, which was a lot. And now, suddenly, there was some kind of computer inside them? A gadget? A scanner? What was he doing?

"Inside car?"

"Yes." He understood. Thank God.

"Office?"

"Yes. I'm sure. They had to be."

"Why?" The beast looked at me then, his attention complete and focused. My entire body tingled with awareness. Was this what he would be like if he had sex with me in his beast's form? Would he be so...intense? "Elena."

My name on his lips was a reprimand, not an endearment. I understood. Here we were in danger, being spied on, watched, and I was daydreaming about having sex with a beast. Feeling him inside me. Having his hands all over me. Touching me. I'd kissed this beast once, in the car, and his lips had been slightly wider, his touch rougher than Tane, the man's, had been. His hard cock had made being on his lap like sitting on top of a long, thick rock. I was still wet. I ached. My breasts were too heavy. Hot. Too sensitive. My mouth was dry. I was trembling and I couldn't seem to stop.

"Tane. I don't know what to do."

His gaze narrowed and he took a deep breath. A soft growl rumbled up through his body, and I knew he could sense what I was feeling. Maybe he could smell the heat between my legs. Maybe he had bionic hearing and knew my pulse was pounding faster than a snare drummer's solo.

He placed the spy gear between his thumb and index finger and squeezed. When he opened his fingers again, nothing but dust remained.

Holy shit. He was a lot stronger than he looked. And he looked like the freaking Hulk. Except sexy and not green.

He placed his fingers under the stream of water filling the tub and washed the dust away. "You live here?"

"Yes. Not here. In another building."

"Watch you there?" the beast asked.

Horror filled my chest. "No. No way." I'd been here for three years, tutoring Abby. George Gregg hadn't shown the slightest interest in me other than as a tool to be used. If he'd been spying on me, I would have found the cameras by now. Because I'd looked. More than once. I'd even ordered one of those special frequency sensors off the Internet. I had no idea if it had actually worked, but I'd scanned my entire suite, found nothing, and felt a lot better after.

I turned off the water and led the way out of Tane's rooms. I didn't come to the main house often. Frankly, neither did Abby nor Mr. Gregg. There was a slightly smaller mansion set back a few hundred paces behind the building I thought of as a castle. That was where I lived. Where Abby lived. Where Mr. Gregg slept when he was home, and where he kept his private office. It was still huge but not *castle* huge.

A little less than ten minutes later Tane's beast followed me into my private suite and closed the door. I locked it, moved a chair in front of the doorknob, and wedged it tight. Not that anyone would dare come in here if Tane was with me. But still...I was on edge, and the dumb chair made me feel better.

"Tane, I—"

"Shhh." He placed his large finger over my lips in an exact mimic of what I'd done to him earlier.

"Fine." He was right. We needed to be sure no one was listening.

I tried to be patient as Tane walked around my private space. He was so big he filled the room. Took it over. He walked slowly and I managed to occasionally catch a glimpse of his eyes going silver or flashing with tiny lightning bolts on the inside. I sat down at my desk and waited. Ten minutes passed. Twenty.

Finally he turned to me and inclined his chin. "Nothing right now."

Suddenly my back felt as if it were made of jelly, and I slumped against my desk. "Thank God." I didn't want to think Mr. Gregg would do that to me. But I wasn't so naive that I dismissed the possibility, either. Not after what we'd found in Tane's guest rooms. And who knew what else my boss had done. We'd had foreign ambassadors, business tycoons, billionaires, politicians, and bankers in the castle as special guests. Dozens of them.

Did George Gregg spy on *all of them?* Or just the aliens? Just Tane?

"I need a new job." My cell phone buzzed, and I checked the screen even as I sensed Tane moving closer. I

had half a dozen texts from Dominique. All asking if I
was okay.

With a smile, I hit the number four and sent it back.

We had a secret code. We'd borrowed the military's
DEFCON system. Five meant all was well. One meant
serious, hell on Earth, trouble. I wasn't reading a book
and eating ice cream, but I wasn't running for my life
either. A two would require an emergency pickup. A
three a phone call. A four meant stand by but don't get
sloppy drunk and forget to check your phone.

Yes, a four seemed appropriate and would keep
Dominique from pounding down my door.

Setting the phone aside, I turned in my chair as Tane
came to stand before me. Slowly he lifted the strap of the
black bag he'd been carrying off his shoulder. Kneeling
on the thick carpet, he opened the bag and removed its
contents.

I gasped.

Mating cuffs. Two big ones for him, and two smaller
ones for me. They were beautiful, elaborately carved with
shifting tones of gold, silver, and pewter. The symbols
were so intertwined they almost looked like they were
moving. Alive.

Once I could tear my gaze from the mating cuffs, I
looked up to find Tane's beast staring at me intently.
Watching. Waiting.

"You think I'm your mate?"

"No. I. Am. Yours. I protect. I serve. I obey. Only you."
The beast spoke in short, distinct bursts. There was no
mistaking his words or his intent. He meant what he was
saying, and that shook me to my soul. I hadn't been loved

in a long time. Not since my parents had died. But was this love? Lust? Alien chemistry? I wanted to say yes more than I'd ever wanted anything in my life.

Holy mother of God. My own mother would be scandalized, turning over in her grave if she knew how fast this thing between Tane and I had gone. My father would smile and tell me to follow my heart. He'd proposed to my mother two weeks after they met.

Guess the blood in my family ran hot.

And true. They'd stayed together until the day they died. As had my grandparents. And my great-grandparents. Divorce was not a thing in my Catholic family. A vow made before God was a vow forever.

I stared at the mating cuffs. They were a vow too. A promise. Unbreakable. Eternal.

I'd known him for a day. Danced with him once. Had sex with him once. But I knew. He was mine, whatever that meant. He was mine and I was keeping him. I'd deal with the rest as it came.

Tane's beast remained on one knee, waiting for me to decide his fate. To accept him as my mate forever or to deny him. Refuse to accept his beast. Refuse to wear the mating cuffs.

He was shaking.

I reached for the first cuff, opened it, and placed it around his wrist. The alien jewelry seemed to close all by itself, so I reached for the second. He held my gaze as I wrapped the gorgeous metal around his wrist.

"You're mine now, beast. Can't change your mind." I smiled at him. I couldn't help it. Joy was bursting through every cell in my body. Joy? Love? Champagne bubbles of happiness in my blood? Whatever it was, these feelings were because of him. My Atlan warlord. My beast.

I snapped the second cuff closed and reached for his face. I rested my palm against his cheek, traced his bottom lip with my thumb. "I hope you know what you're doing, because I won't give you up."

Eyes gone dark, he made quick work of placing the matching cuffs on my wrists. They were surprisingly light and comfortable. They didn't dig into my skin or feel heavy. Once I got used to them, I wouldn't even notice I was wearing them. Which was good, because according to what I'd read, mated Atlan couples rarely took them off.

The beast reached for me, tried to release the small, square buttons on my navy jacket, but his hands shook too badly for the delicate work.

Gently pushing his hands out of the way, I made quick work of the buttons and removed my jacket. I tossed it on the floor and tugged the hem of my silk blouse free from the waist of my skirt. My high heels caught on the thick pile carpeting, so I kicked them off.

Tane looked down immediately, a grin on his face. "Orange."

"What?"

"Wondered." He looked back up at me. "Orange paint."

He was talking about my toenails. Had he truly been so attuned to me that he knew I'd painted my toenails this morning before driving into the city? I pulled the blouse off over my head and tossed it as well. "How did you know I painted them?"

He lifted one hand and tapped a finger to his nose,

but he was no longer looking at my face. His focus had moved to my lace bra. Pastel pink. It was one of my favorites, and I wore it and the matching panties when I needed to feel especially confident. Like today.

God, if he was that sensitive to smell, I'd have to shower twice a day. Brush my teeth every hour. How was I going to—

His lips closed around my nipple, lace and all. His palm rubbed the outer edge of my thigh, sneaking up inside my skirt. He was using his other hand to wrap around my back, lift me from the chair. I expected him to carry me to the bed or lay me down on the floor. Instead he carried me to my standing work desk and shoved the papers aside with one sweep of his arm. He settled me on the hard surface and stood between my legs staring down at me like he was a god and I was an offering sprawled across the altar.

He bent down and kissed my inner thigh, moving my skirt up bit by bit as he went.

I was on my back, his hot breath on my skin, and my entire being exploded with lust. This was where I wanted to be. I wanted him over me. Inside me. Driving me crazy. Making me forget everything but him.

He wiggled the fabric of my skirt up to my waist. Kissed the slight mound between my legs through my lace panties. His hands lingered at my waist, holding me in place. I was at his mercy. Utterly. Completely. His tongue moved over my clit.

Breathing became an act of extreme will.

Shit.

"No. No. No. Stop!" I wiggled until I could get my bare foot up on his shoulder and push. "Tane, stop."

Tane froze as if I'd splashed cold water on his head. Too bad. This was not happening again. Already I could feel the fire between us building into an inferno. Any minute now one or both of us was going to be totally out of control. Then it would be too late.

9

HE LIFTED his gaze to meet mine, the beast's eyes filled with confusion. "What wrong?"

So direct and to the point, my beast. I liked the sound of that. My. Beast.

My *naked* beast sounded even better. I held his gaze and smiled at him.

"Take off your clothes. All of them. We are not having sex with our clothes on. I want skin, mister. I want you naked this time. Totally, completely naked."

I had never heard a beast laugh, but the rumble coming from Tane was laughter, no doubt. "Bossy female."

"Get used to it." I was smiling; I couldn't help it. "Naked, Tane. Like right now."

His gaze turned serious, darker. "Naked." His fingertips moved along the hem of my skirt, and he ripped the seam as easily as I would tear a tissue. When he hooked his thumb in my favorite pink lace panties, I squirmed fast.

"Oh no. You are not ruining these panties."

His brow lifted and I knew I had about three seconds to get them off my body if I wanted to save them. I had them off in two. My bra hit the floor immediately after. I was naked. He was not.

"Your turn."

He took a step back, and I watched, fascinated, as he revealed his massive physique to me. First his chest. Never-ending muscles. Rock-hard abs. And strange silver streaks that almost looked like threads running through his skin in a grid. I'd never seen anything like it, but it didn't distract from his sexual appeal. He still looked like a god come to life. When he dropped his pants and I could see the rest of him, I became a bit dizzy.

I knew Tane's cock was big. I'd felt it once already. But the beast's private parts?

Good grief. That was not going to fit inside me. It just wasn't. No way. Not possible. It was too big. Too hard. Too...

I lost my train of thought as Tane's mouth closed over my pussy like he was devouring me whole. His fingers soon found a rhythm to match his tongue, and my back arched up off the desk as he pushed me into an orgasm harder and faster than I'd ever thought possible.

He grunted with satisfaction, then shook his head. "Too tight."

Adding another finger to my core, he moved three fingers in and out of my body, slowly, building the tension as he kissed and licked at my breasts, my stomach. He made his way back down to my core and sucked the hard nub into his mouth, used his lips and tongue to suck and release my clit in a rapid-fire pace.

My hands fisted at my sides. Screw that. I buried them in his hair and pulled his head down harder. I wanted more pressure. Faster. Fingers deeper.

More.

I came with a primitive cry I'd never heard before, not from my throat. But I could not stop. The orgasm went on and on. Tane moved quickly, positioning himself at my entrance and thrusting forward slowly, stretching my pulsing muscles with his hard length, pushing me higher.

When he was buried deep, he stared down at me, waiting for me to recover, to look at him.

"Mine."

One word, that's what I got from him, and then he was pumping into me like the beast he was. I loved it, every hard thrust, every grunt. I loved the way his fingers dug into the flesh of my hips as he held me in place. Loved the way my breasts jiggled as he rocked my entire body.

My pussy was so tight, so swollen, so damn sensitive that just the friction of his huge cock had me on the edge. I reached down and rubbed my clit with my fingers as he fucked me. Once. Twice.

My orgasm roared through me like a rocket launch.

He fucked me hard. Deep. I didn't know where to put my hands. I settled with holding on to his wrists. The warm strength of his hands and the solid reminder of the mating cuffs filled me with emotions I wasn't prepared to feel.

I felt safe. Like I belonged to something other than myself. I felt important. Cherished.

There would be no escaping this alien, this beast, and I didn't want to. I was his forever, the thought releasing all the tension from my chest, from my body. I relaxed into his thrusts, went soft, gave him everything. Let him take what he wanted. Let him fuck me. Fill me. Bury his body in mine and find his own peace.

He came with a roar that would have caused a car alarm to go off if we'd been outside. I loved the sound, the emotion behind it, the intensity of his release. I did that to him. Me. The thought was crazy and exciting and terrifying all at the same time. Me! Mated to an alien beast. Forever.

Where were we going to live? Did he even want to live with me? How did alien relationships work? I had no idea. What had I done? What, exactly, had I agreed to when I put on these stupid, romantic mating cuffs?

"Tane?" I was lying on a desk, Tane's cock still inside me, and I was about to go into a full-blown panic.

His beast grumbled a response, busy exploring my body with his hands, petting me, tracing my curves. Which was really, really nice, but...

"Tane?"

"Busy." The beast was cupping my breasts, running a thumb over each nipple, watching my breathing change, my nipples peak. His cock, still inside me, remained hard. One shift of his hips and we'd be at it again.

A jolt of pleasure shot from my nipples to my core, and I moaned as he pulled out of my body slowly. Thrust back inside fast. Again. Slower. And faster.

I shuddered and wrapped my legs around his hips,

locked him to my body. I wanted him, all right, but I didn't want to be lying on this stupid, hard, too small desk.

"I want to be on top."

My beast froze midstroke, a shudder passing through him. I watched him struggle to control himself, and then he was lifting me in his arms and carrying me to the bed.

When we arrived, it was Tane who laid down on his back and settled me on top of him. Not the beast.

He was reclined, his cock still inside me as I laid my hands on his chest and looked down at my man. My mate. "What happened to the beast?"

"Instincts won't allow him to fuck you like this. It's too dangerous. He feels too vulnerable to attack. A beast never fucks unless he's standing up, in full control, so he can defend his mate at any moment."

I sank down, taking him all the way inside. It hurt, and it felt amazing at the same time. God, he was huge. "Why didn't he just say no then? I could have waited to have you like this."

Tane shook his head and lifted one hand to cup my cheek. "You don't understand yet, Elena, but you will. You ask; I provide. I will do anything in my power to give you what you need and to make you happy. And so will my beast. He's claimed you now, and you accepted him. You wear the mating cuffs. You are the only person in the universe he will listen to now. He's yours, completely, just like I am."

I traced a line of silver from his shoulder to his stomach, enjoyed the way his cock jumped inside me, the way he shivered. "This is crazy, Tane. You know that, right?

How can you fall in love so fast? How do you know I'm the right woman?"

He grabbed my wandering hand and pulled it over his heart, held it there. "This is not human love. This is more. The beast chose you as his mate. From that moment, his life was in your hands. My life. My soul. My everything."

He lifted his hips, his cock shifting inside me. I moaned and dropped my cheek into his palm. "Okay. I don't understand, but I trust you."

"I'll make you happy. I will take care of you. You are the only thing that matters to me now."

"You are so intense."

"I think you like intense." He moved quickly, placing his hands on my hips so he could lift me up. Gravity took me back down, the slide of my wet core over his cock pure bliss.

"Do that again."

He did. Over. And over. Until I lost control. Until I sobbed. Until I was weak from exhaustion and collapsed across his chest. When I was cold, he covered me with a blanket. When I started to worry, he stroked my back until I calmed. How he knew what I was feeling, I wasn't sure. Smell? Acute observation? It wasn't like I was trying to hide anything.

He was amazing. That was that. Gorgeous. And mine. He would never cheat on me, and he would never leave me.

I was totally keeping him. Tane *and* his beast.

Mine. The mating cuffs were proof of that. Of course, so was the mess we'd made coming all over each other for the last hour. I was now basically married to an alien.

Okay.

Alien husband aside, what were we going to do about Mr. Gregg, our eavesdropping host?

———

TANE, Three days later

WE DID NOT LEAVE Elena's rooms for three days.

I fucked her.

The beast fucked her.

We took long, hot bubble baths in a tub large enough to fit me and my beast both, with enough room to hold Elena on our lap and smear her with bubbles.

The young female, Abby, became an ally. Elena used her cell phone to order food delivered to the estate. Abby would accept the delivery and bring the sustenance to our door. She would then send a text to Elena when it was safe to open the door and grab our meal.

I could have stayed with her in this isolated bit of heaven for weeks. My beautiful, soft, curvy mate. She was more than I'd dared hope for. More than I'd imagined. Kind. Funny. Quick to laugh. Adventurous. Passionate. All I needed was to look at her and my body was hard and ready, eager to touch her. Fuck her. Claim her again. The sight of my mating cuffs on her wrists filled me with a contentment I'd never known.

Elena, the fairy-tale princess from the ball, was all mine, and I could not believe my good fortune.

I checked in with Bahre and the others as well. They were happy for me, especially Quinn, who talked nonstop in the background while I was speaking to Bahre, letting him know where I was and who I was with.

Midmorning sunlight made her bedroom glow, the light made warmer by the sheer orange and beige fabric covering her windows. I'd taken her already this morning, my beast choosing to take over halfway through our mating. Elena had looked at him and laughed as he'd carried her to the wall and held her in place with her back against the smooth, patterned wallpaper. He fucked her there, made her beg, made her come before he filled her with his seed and allowed me to return.

He was as hungry for her as I. Every moment. Every breath. Elena was the only thing either I or my beast thought about. Wanted. Needed. The rest of the world could go fuck itself for all I cared. I had my mate now. Nothing else mattered.

Nothing.

"What do you want to do today?" Elena lay sprawled across my chest, her naked thighs covering mine as I held her close, exactly where she was meant to be. In my arms. With me. Next to me. "We can't just hide in my room for the rest of our lives."

"We are not hiding, mate. I am fucking you and giving you so much pleasure you won't be able to resist me."

She laughed. "Mission accomplished. I surrender." She leaned down and placed a kiss on my chest, the small act one that made my heart swell with warmth. "I cannot resist you."

Mine. The beast's possessive nature swamped my mind, but I had no intention of fighting him. Not about this.

"I require proof." Without warning, I rolled Elena beneath me on the bed and filled her pussy with one well-aimed thrust of my hips. My cock was hard and eager for her despite the fact that I'd fucked her less than an hour earlier.

She shuddered, her legs opening to accept me. She wrapped her arms around my neck and arched her back, shifting her hips to take me deeper with a soft moan I'd come to need more than I needed air to breathe. "Oh God. You are insatiable."

"Do you wish me to stop?"

"Don't you dare." She gasped her command as I slowly fucked her, moving in and out of her body in a leisurely pace designed to drive her to the brink. When she couldn't take any more, when I had pushed her body beyond endurance, she would beg. She would demand. She would thrash and groan and dig her fingernails into my back.

Then I would fuck her hard. Fast. Make her scream. Give her release.

I'd become obsessed with giving her pleasure. Another new and unexpected joy.

We moved together, taking our time, letting the heat build. When I knew she was ready, primed for an orgasm that would make her cry out, I thrust harder and faster, moved my hand between our bodies to stroke her clit until she cried out, her pussy pulsing around my hard cock, clamping down on me like a vise that forced the seed from my body as my beast growled.

He would be next. But our mate collapsed on the bed when her orgasm faded. Her eyelids drifted closed. "You're going to kill me."

"Then you must rest. I will draw a bath. The beast wants to spread soap all over your skin."

"Beast, you are such an animal. You just want to get me all slippery and wet."

I grinned. "You have discovered his secret."

Her hand came up to rest on my cheek and her eyes were full of something soft and vulnerable. I froze, captivated by that look. "It's not a secret. I have him figured out."

"You do? And what do you know about your beast?"

"He is obsessed with getting me naked."

I burst out laughing. "You do have him figured out after all."

She grinned up at me, but a soft groan escaped her and I shifted my weight immediately, pulling my cock from her body. "Are you unwell?"

"Just sore. I don't usually spend three days...you know. And you aren't exactly small."

Fuck. I was failing her already. "I will take you to Bahre's home at once and treat you with a ReGen wand. My apologies, mate. Can you forgive me?"

"For what? And what's a ReGen wand?"

"I am not caring for you properly. I should have anticipated your discomfort. And a ReGen wand is Coalition technology that will heal your body from the inside out in just a few minutes."

"What? You guys can do that?"

"Of course."

She froze, her body going stiff beneath me. "What else do you guys have that you aren't sharing with us?"

10

Sensing danger, I chose my words carefully. "There are many technologies we possess that were deemed too dangerous to share with humans at this time. Including the ReGen technology. It can be used to harm as easily as it can be used to heal. Many leaders among the Coalition of Planets do not believe Earth's leaders will make responsible decisions if given this technology."

"You think we'd use it to kill each other." Her words were more statement than question.

"Yes."

She blinked slowly, considering. "You're probably right. I hate it, but you're right. People suck."

"What do they suck upon?"

Elena's dark brown eyes practically glowed with

warmth. "They just suck in general. They don't actually put their mouths on something and suck on it."

I did not understand, but I was not going to make an ass of myself by asking again. "If you say so. I have not seen this sucking."

"Oh yes, you have!" Now she was laughing outright. "Chet Bosworth ring any bells? He's greedy and ambitious and will do or say anything to get more attention. He sucks."

"On what? I have not seen him with his mouth on anything other than a microphone."

"Oh my God. You are impossible."

I carried my giggling female to the bathing room and filled the bathtub with warm water and bubbles. I did not have a ReGen wand, but I could soothe her body with a heated bath.

We settled in the water, and my beast rushed to the surface almost immediately. Elena turned away, grabbed the soap, and when she turned back to face me, she was looking at the beast.

"Well, hello there, big guy."

The beast held out his hand for the soap. Elena shook her head. "Nope. My turn."

If my beast had not been totally enamored of our mate before, ten minutes later he was slick with soap, soothed by small feminine hands, and completely drunk on our mate's attention. Pathetic.

I was a bit jealous.

Elena rinsed the beast and then sat on his lap giving him long, lingering, soul-stealing kisses. Not demanding or sexual. Giving. Adoring. Gentle.

I shoved the beast back inside and took over. Elena

was grinning at me again.

"Couldn't take it, huh?"

"Couldn't take what?"

"The beast getting all the attention."

"I am the beast. These kisses are mine."

She placed her lips against mine. "Don't worry, Tane, I've got enough kisses for both of you."

A warlord should be strong. Fierce. Brutal. Merciless. And I was all those things. But not with her. Not now. "Elena." Her name was all I could manage to get past the tight knot in my throat.

"Shhh." She kissed me into silence and I allowed it. Held her. My peace and my salvation. I understood now why a beast would choose death when a mate was lost.

I would not choose to go on without her.

We lingered in the bath, but not nearly long enough. My mate was hungry, and I had made her pussy sore. The knowledge that she was in pain plagued me. She would be healed as soon as possible.

Dressed and ready to face the world once more, we both turned as our cell phones chimed at nearly the same time. Elena read her text message, and her face drained of all color. "Oh shit. It's Dominique. DEFCON 1."

"Is she in trouble?"

Elena shook her head. "No. We are."

"What is the issue?"

"I don't know. She sent me a link..." Elena's voice faded. She pressed her fingertip to her cell phone's screen and waited. A few seconds later I heard her voice, Elena's voice, coming not from her body, but from the cell phone.

"No. No. Stop!"

There were a series of growling sounds that I recognized as my own.

Her screams of pleasure came next, but they were not quite right, as if they had been modified. Altered somehow.

"No. Stop! Stop!" The same words were repeated, the exact same words from earlier in the recording, played again, in a different order.

That was followed by the distinct sounds of Elena sobbing the word *please* over and over again. I remembered the moment well, as my beautiful mate had been begging me to give her an orgasm, but the sequence of events sounded wrong.

More sobbing.

"Tane. Stop! No. No."

What the fuck? I moved to look at the phone screen over Elena's shoulder as a serious-looking female sitting in front of what looked like a news anchor's desk spoke with an image of me fucking my female frozen in a rectangular digital screen next to her talking head.

The strange woman's voice sounded serious, angry. *"I don't want to believe it, but that is raw footage from a scene that played out after the now infamous Cinderella Ball. It appears that the alien from Atlan, Warlord Tane, was repeatedly told to stop having sexual relations with Miss Elena Garcia and did not comply. Are we looking at possible sexual assault charges, David? Because where I come from, when a woman says no, she means no. Based on what we just saw with our own eyes, we have video footage of a brutal sexual assault, as it happened."*

What. The. Fuck?

"Oh my God. Oh my God. How did this happen? How

did they...?" Elena paused midsentence and looked around her room with tears in her eyes. "Tane? When you checked the room, would your super senses know if a video camera was here, even if it wasn't on?"

Fuck.

Elena looked at me and must have realized the answer based on my expression. I clarified anyway. "I was only looking for live frequencies and active electrical current. If they had cameras here that were not on at the time, they would have registered as dead weight, just like everything else in the room."

"Oh God. What are we going to do?"

I pulled her close and held her shaking frame to my chest. "You are going to pack a bag with anything important to you, and we are going to leave this place."

"Okay." Elena nodded her head against me, her tears soaking my shirt. Gods be damned, I was going to kill whoever was responsible.

"Make sure you take anything you care about. You are not coming back here. Ever."

"What about Abby?"

"Trust me, mate. Pack your things. I will take care of this."

Elena moved in fits and starts, her body stiff, tears appearing and disappearing with regularity. I called Bahre while she packed.

"Have you seen the video?"

"Yes. The police were here looking for you. Get the fuck out of there. I'm sure they are already on their way."

I took a deep breath. "Bahre, you know I didn't—"

"Don't fucking insult me. I know that."

Shocked by the weight that lifted from my chest, I

turned as Elena zipped a suitcase closed and faced me with her hands on her hips.

"Okay. I'm ready."

"We're on our way to you." I hung up and looked at Elena. "Do you have a car?" Never again would I accept a ride from a human. Now I was stranded with no vehicle and no way to escape with my mate. What the fuck had I been thinking the last few days? Why had I not worried about her safety?

Because I'd been too busy being kissed and fucked and coddled by my female. I'd been weak. And I'd failed her because of it.

Elena shook her head. "No. Never needed one." She reached for her cell phone. "But Abby does."

"Will she help us?"

"I don't know. I'll text her." Elena's fingers flew across her phone. Less than a minute later, Abby was pounding on the bedroom door.

"Elena? It's me! I hate him. I hate him so much! Let me in!"

Elena opened the door to find Abby standing in the hallway, her young face streaked with tears.

"I hate him. I'm so sorry. I didn't know he would do this to you. I can't believe it."

Elena pulled the young girl into her arms and wrapped her in a tight hug. "It's not your fault."

"I'm so sorry." Abby sobbed. "I heard him talking to that stupid paparazzi, and I didn't say anything. They have another video too. Something about a fight club and some guy getting killed by some Prillons."

Fuck. Was she talking about Maxus and the night the Hive Trackers had shown up at his fight club? There had been a small battle that night. Blood. And a dead human.

"What fight club? What did you hear?" I tried to keep my voice calm so as not to frighten the girl, but I was afraid I knew exactly what she was talking about.

"The video was taken in Miami a few weeks ago. It was an underground club. Illegal, you know? One of those places where the guys fight with no rules? Anyway, somebody died and my dad wants to use the footage against you. Well, not just you. All the aliens."

Fuck. This was a problem. Maxus and Vivian. Snook's illegal fighting club. The encounter we'd had with the Hive Trackers there, and the human the Hive had killed trying to get to Vivian to take her hostage. Their plan had failed. All the Trackers were dead except two, and those two Prillon warriors had already been transported to The Colony so that Dr. Surnen could attempt to save them.

But these ladies knew none of that history.

Abby lifted her head from Elena's shoulder and looked up at me. "Do you know what they are talking about?"

"Perhaps." I could not lie to the girl, but she did not need to know details.

"Perhaps? A fighter called the White Wolf—who was actually an alien—and he wasn't supposed to be living here, but he was hiding, like illegally, breaking all the human and alien laws. He was a beast, Tane. Like you. And a paramedic that died, or maybe it was a driver? Someone was murdered and they covered it up. Daddy said he was going to show the proof to some senator. He doesn't want the Coalition here. He hates all the aliens. Badly."

"When was this?" Elena asked. "When did you hear this conversation?"

Abby wiped her cheeks. "A week ago maybe?"

"Where is your father now?" I asked.

"I don't know. Washington? New York? Some senator's house? He's not here. He's never here."

Elena pulled the girl into another hug and looked up at me over the girl's shoulder. "What are we going to do?"

I hated every word that was about to come out of my mouth.

"Abby? Can you get a copy of that video? The one where the human is killed?"

"Maybe. I can try. I am friends with the security team. They might give it to me. Or help me find it."

"Excellent." I cleared my throat. "And I need you to get all the video taken inside Elena's room for the last three days. Get a copy of the data and delete them from your father's system. Can you do that?"

"I'll try."

"Find a way. For Elena." I looked at my mate, at her pale face and trembling hands. I fought back the urge to kill Abby's father, the woman on the news screen, and anyone who had watched that abomination and distortion of the pleasure Elena and I had found together.

Abby looked at Elena and smacked her on the shoulder. "Girlfriend, you didn't tell me you were going to make a sex tape."

Elena choked on a laugh that wasn't really a laugh. "Right? Next time I'll try to give you a heads-up."

Abby nodded. "Don't worry too much, okay? I know the security guys can get the footage from your rooms for me. A few of them are total computer nerds. They help me spy on Daddy all the time."

"They do?" Elena sounded shocked.

"Duh. How do you think I always know the perfect time to ask him for something?"

This time Elena's laughter was real. "Okay. So get your hands on the sex tape, please. And you know—Tane didn't—"

Abby shushed her. "Shhh. I know. I spy on you, too."

"Abigail Elizabeth Gregg!" Elena's tone was fierce—and disapproving.

Abby shrugged, totally unapologetic. "Hey, it's better than watching porn, right? At least your man makes sure you enjoy yourself, if you know what I mean." The young lady's face turned bright red as she held out a set of keys. "God. So embarrassing. Take my car. Get out of here. I'll try to get the videos." She looked up at me. "All of them."

"Text me," Elena ordered.

"Okay. I will." Abby pulled her own cell phone from the pocket of her sweatpants and glanced down at the screen. "Oh shit. That's my guy. There's a line of cops waiting at the front gate." She glanced up at Elena. "Better go out the back."

Elena kissed the girl on the cheek and gave her one more fast, tight hug. "Thank you."

"You're the only family I have, Elena. You and Dominique. So go. Get the hell out of here."

I grabbed Elena's suitcase and gave Abby a bow of respect and thanks as we left our false paradise behind.

"Wait! Tane!"

I turned back to find Abby running toward me. She

barreled into me, then wrapped her arms around me and gave me a very tight hug. "Take care of her, okay?"

"She is mine, Abby. Nothing will ever harm her again."

"Okay. Good. I'll stall the cops." Abby released me and took two steps back. "You aliens aren't so bad, you know?"

I grinned. "Thank you." Approval from a human girl barely more than a child. Why did her affection please me so?

Because she belonged to Elena. And Elena was mine.

The sound of police sirens leaked into the hallway. Multiple sirens. A fucking large number of vehicles were heading this way.

"Tane! We gotta go!"

11

ABBY'S CAR was better suited to a racetrack than the road, but the windows were tinted so dark no one would be able to see inside, and I was feeling aggressive. The roar of the overpowered engine suited me just fine.

Next to me in the passenger seat, poor Tane had his long legs folded up like a pretzel and his neck bent forward, his chin nearly touching his chest. No matter what he did, the back of his head rubbed the ceiling. There was no way he could drive. None. Which made him curse and demand we take another vehicle. Unfortunately for my man, there were no other vehicles available. Mr. Gregg kept every set of keys, other than Abby's, in his personal safe.

Getting Tane inside this car was like trying to stuff a giant teddy bear into a shoebox. He simply did not fit.

I glanced at him out of the corner of my eye and found him watching me. "What?"

"I have failed you, Elena. I will never forgive myself for that failure, but I will kill George Gregg."

The biggest man I'd ever met was crammed into a clown car and threatening to kill a bitter old man I didn't care about?

God, he was adorable. Big. Scary. Tough. Alien.

Adorable.

I hit the garage door button that would open the entrance to the secret tunnel I'd been barreling through like a big yellow bullet. The car sped out from behind what appeared, to the outside world, to be a side road leading nowhere. I hit the gas, speeding up as we left the Gregg estate behind, accelerating until the vegetation along the side of the road was nothing more than a blur.

Of course it was a blur anyway because I hadn't had time to put in my contacts and my glasses had been broken for weeks. I could see. Mostly. Well enough not to drive us into a ditch.

A sharp curve appeared in the road ahead, and I had to downshift and hit the brakes to keep the tires from lifting off the pavement.

"Elena, slow down." The words were a command, nothing less.

I wanted to argue, but he was right. "Sorry, I drive aggressive when I'm angry."

"Then you will cease being angry."

"Says the warlord who just threatened to kill a man." We came out of the S curves, and I hit the gas again, went a bit faster, just to drive Tane a little bit crazy. "Which you can't do, by the way. You can't touch him. If you do, you'll give him exactly what he needs to get you guys kicked off the planet."

"Hmmm." My beast stared ahead as if considering my words, but I had a feeling that once he got together with his alien buddies, all bets would be off. They didn't seem to be the kind of guys—aliens—who would listen to reason when it came to someone harming one of their mates. Their women.

Which was *me*. Holy shit, that was me.

Yes, the sex tape made me angry, made me want to curl into a ball and cry, made me want to wring Mr. Gregg's neck myself, but another, bigger part of me was numb about the whole thing. My parents were dead. Dominique was the only friend I had, other than Abby, whose opinions mattered, and they both knew the truth. The video was a lie. A flat-out, bald-faced lie.

But...what about the *other* video Abby had mentioned? The one where the aliens had apparently killed a man? And covered it up?

That was going to cause problems. Big, big problems, if it was true.

Was it true? And if so, why would they do that? What the hell was going on? What did Tane know?

The secret tunnel had dumped us onto the road more than half a mile away from the line of flashing lights waiting to enter the Gregg compound. I had driven us a good distance. I couldn't see the cop cars' lights anymore. And no one appeared to be following us. I was not prepared to drive straight to some alien's house where I'd be outnumbered and outgunned. Even alone with Tane, I was out of my league. What would I do with five or six of these big aliens around?

I turned onto a small side road that I knew ended at a large drainage ditch, and slowed down enough that Tane's head wasn't actually threatening to punch a hole in the roof of Abby's little yellow sports car every time one of the tires hit a hole in the dirt road.

I hit the brakes, and the car slid forward a couple feet on loose gravel. I was out of the car and pacing seconds after it stopped, the dirt and rock crunching under my feet. A wire fence separated me from a large ditch full of dark, swampy water. It smelled like swamp, all right. And alligators, most likely. This was the kind of place the ancient reptiles really, really loved.

Squinting, I peered down into the ditch but didn't see one of the creatures sunning itself on the embankment or a nose poking up through the top of the water. Seemed safe enough. "I really should have put in my contacts."

"What did you just say?"

"I'm nearsighted, you know? I mean, I can drive without them. Technically I'm not supposed to, but I can see the road. Just can't tell if all the green is just grass or if there is an alligator hiding in there." I put my hands on my hips. "Whatever."

A stupid reptile was the least of my problems at the moment. The more I thought about everything, the worse the situation became.

Tane took a bit longer unfolding himself from the too small passenger seat, but he joined me soon enough, standing at the hood the car with his arms crossed over his chest, watching me walk back and forth in front of him like a wind-up toy.

"You cannot see properly?"

"It's okay."

"You were driving at high speeds without seeing where you were going?"

"It's just blurry, that's all. It's fine. I'm fine." I couldn't stop walking. Back and forth. Back and forth. I felt like if I stopped, I might explode.

Tane reached for me, and he took a fistful of my hair, gently angled my face up so I was forced to look him in the eye. "Do not make me spank you, female."

Oh. My. God. My panties were dripping wet. I wanted that sting on my ass. So badly.

Tane's gaze turned dark as he assessed my reaction. "Not a threat. I will remember that."

Was I still breathing? Had my heart stopped? Was I numb or so overly stimulated that my nervous system was overloaded?

I closed my eyes and tugged against the strong hand securely buried in my hair. Tugged just enough to make my scalp burn. Breathed in Tane's scent. His skin. His breath. Yes. Definitely, yes. Still alive.

"What are you doing, Elena? Why have we stopped here? We need to get to Bahre's home as quickly as possible. You will be safe there."

"I'm safe here." We were perfectly safe. No people. No cars. No video cameras. "Except maybe satellites. Do you think they are taking our picture right now?"

"What are you talking about?"

"Video. You know. Do you think they can get us here?"

"No. But you will get in that car and drive us to Warlord Bahre's home. It is heavily fortified, guarded by Atlan and Prillon both. And we secured the area with our own technology. It is probably the safest place on Earth right now."

"Let's just stay here."

"Elena."

That voice. Damn it. He could melt me into a puddle with the voice.

I threw my hands in the air and tried to ignore the little thrill that shot through me when I noticed how beautiful the mating cuffs looked when the sunlight hit them just right. Truly gorgeous. Like sparkling diamonds or— "No. No. No. You are not going to distract me."

"I have done nothing but ask you a question."

"No. Not you." I held the mating cuffs on my wrists up, in front of my face, but the effect was totally lost on him. "Okay. Yes, you. Kind of. But that's not what I'm talking about."

Tane blinked. Slowly. He released me, his hand slipping from the back of my head to my shoulder. "Elena, little one, you need to slow down."

So maybe I'd been overwhelmed back at the house. Or numb? Delayed reaction? I had no idea where the scream came from, but the next thing I knew, I had turned toward the alligator ditch and scared the birds into a flurry of agitated flight from the trees. Tane's arms wrapped me up tight as raw fury exploded from my chest.

How *dare* he record me in my own goddamn, fucking bedroom? And making it look like Tane raped me? Releasing the tape to the vultures all over social media?

"I'm going to kill him. I'm going to rip his balls off his old, frail fucking body and shove them down his throat. I'm going to claw his eyes out of his skull and stomp them under my heels." My voice was garbled, and I wasn't sure if it was caused by rage or my sobbing. Probably both. "How dare he do that to you?"

Tane had been holding me, running his hands up and down my back as I ranted. He stopped. "What did you just say?"

I smacked my fists into his chest. "How dare he do that to you? Fuck him. That motherfucker, piece of shit, billionaire asshole." I threw in a few heated curses in my parent's native Spanish for good measure.

Tane placed his hands on either side of my face. "Elena, stop."

I couldn't. I had a thousand different emotions exploding inside me with nowhere to go. "I can't. I hate him. Hate what he did to you. I knew it was too good to be true. I knew it! He's going to ruin everything. I don't want to go back to the way I was before. I can't do that. I just can't."

"Elena."

"I want to kick him in the face. He's ruining everything!"

"Elena."

"And did you guys kill someone and cover it up? Because that's bad, Tane. Really, really bad. You could go to jail. Who was it? Why would you do that? Why would you do something that stupid?"

Was that wailing sound coming from me?

"Elena!"

"What?" My gaze finally settled in one place, locked onto Tane's face. His big, gorgeous, sexy-as-hell face. "What?"

"Stop. I'm going to take care of this. He can't hurt you, and he can't ruin anything. You are mine."

Oh, this naive alien had no idea what a viral sex video could do. Or a snuff film? *Jesus, Mary, and Joseph.* There weren't enough candles in the world to pray that one away.

Did they really have video of the Atlans killing a human? Shit. So bad.

"No no no. This is so bad." I shook my head, my entire body trembling. "This is a total disaster. Oh my God. What are we going to do? They'll put you in jail. Or maybe not. Maybe they'll lock you away in some military prison and I'll never see you again. They'll beat you and you'll die in there. You'll die and I won't even know what happened to you." I was hyperventilating. Was there a brown paper bag somewhere I could breathe into?

I slammed my flattened palm against my upper chest to give myself something concrete to anchor myself. My thoughts were like a hurricane inside my skull, and they wouldn't stop spinning. "I think I'm going to pass out."

"That's it." Moving fast, Tane lifted me and carried me back to the car. I thought he was going to open the door and tell me to get inside. Instead he draped my chest over the car roof and pulled my pants down and off, tossing them—along with my now ruined red panties—onto the hood of the car.

"What are you—"

A moan replaced my words as he worked two fingers inside my body. I was wet instantly, the sunshine and breeze making me even more attuned to his touch.

"Tane, we can't—"

His hand fisted in my hair, and he gently tugged until my chin was up, off the car, and my scalp stung—just enough. "Mate, you will stop talking. Now."

"But—"

A growl sounded from behind me, and I knew Tane's beast had taken over.

The beast was here, and I responded instinctively, just like a small, weak animal with a predator at my back. He was in control now. My fate was in his hands. There was nothing I could do...

Oh God, yes. I could let go now. Let him take care of me.

Every bit of nervous energy twisted into lust. Heat. Need. My entire body shivered as it welcomed Tane's blatant redirection. Desire was better than fear. Better than rage. Just...better.

Tane's beast spoke to me, the low timbre of his voice making me melt into a puddle of want.

"Mate. Fuck you. Now. No talking. Yes?" The beast moved his fingers in and out of my body, waiting for me to answer him. I was already on the edge, my orgasm building. I wanted him inside me. Now. I didn't want the train wreck that was my mind right now to be in charge. I wanted...him.

"Yes."

He filled me from behind in one smooth motion, the beast's huge cock making me cry out as he thrust deep, not giving me a chance to think too much or change my mind. My head emptied of all thought, all sensation but him. His huge hands on my ass. His massive cock pumping in and out of my body. My breasts rubbed along the roof of Abby's car through my thin shirt and bra, the hard metal making it impossible to escape Tane's pounding rhythm. There was no give in him, no mercy.

I didn't want any. I wanted to be completely taken. I

wanted to forget everything and simply feel. This was raw lust. Sex. A release we both needed.

I came first, my orgasm making me shout in relief. In anguish and pleasure in equal measure. I couldn't get enough of his cock. I couldn't take another thrust of his hips, and at the same time, I never wanted his aggressive pounding to end.

His orgasm followed in seconds, his cock pulsing and filling me with spurts of his seed. The beast draped his torso over me, covered me like a blanket, his hands on top of mine, his body still buried deep as he pressed me up against the car. The beast held me captive for long minutes, his face and neck close enough that all I had to do to kiss his cheek was turn my head.

So I did. I kissed him quietly, over and over. Silently thanked him and tried to let him know I was falling totally and madly in love with him.

I was expecting a lot from those kisses.

He didn't move. He accepted my affection with his eyes closed, our bodies locked together. I wasn't sure how long he intended to stay like this. Was he fighting for control of his emotions, like me, or just enjoying the warm breeze and fresh air? We were stuck together, his seed dripping down my thigh in broad daylight, in the middle of nowhere.

I'd never felt so safe as I did with him all over me. Inside me. Bossy and sexy and beastly. Maybe we could just stay here forever.

I should have kept my proverbial mouth shut because the moment I thought the words, Tane pulled his hard length from my body and settled me on my feet. He turned me to face him, and it was the man I faced, not the beast.

"Better?"

"Yes." I could have lied, but why bother? He already knew the truth. My panic phase had passed, and I was back to unsure, upset, and sad. "Why are people so mean? Why would anyone do that to you? To us?"

He cupped my cheek and kissed me gently. "I don't know. But I promise you, Elena, that man will never hurt you again."

Short of committing cold-blooded murder, I wasn't sure how Tane would keep that promise, but I nodded to let him know I understood he meant what he said.

Tane grabbed what was left of my panties. Kneeling down, he used the soft material to wipe his seed from my thighs and help me clean up. Then he assisted me as I put my pants back on—minus the ripped panties. RIP. Only then did he make sure his own clothes were put to rights.

How could he turn into a beast and fuck my brains out one minute, then be so gentle the next?

He wasn't real. He couldn't be real. No man was this perfect.

But then, he wasn't a man, was he? He was an alien. A beast.

My beast, I quickly reminded myself. I had the mating cuffs and the sore pussy to prove it.

I let Tane take over, my mind numb, my body depleted. I was in shock. Logically I knew that. Didn't make it any easier to accept. I hated being like this. Weak and out of control. Scared.

Tane made a quick call to Bahre, and then he was

holding me in his arms, rocking me against his chest as we stood quietly and listened to the wind and the birds. The cavalry arrived about half an hour later. Three large black SUVs pulled up behind Abby's tiny car, and a handful of scary aliens exited the vehicles. The Atlans Bahre, Kai, and Egon I recognized from advertisements for the *Bachelor Beast* television show. There were also two of the Prillon guards Dominique liked so much dressed in black, as well as two human men in similar uniforms.

"What kind of uniform is that?" I asked. The guards at the Cinderella Ball had been wearing them as well, but I'd never seen anything like them anywhere else.

"Coalition Fleet, my lady," one of the Prillons answered.

Tane nodded to one of the humans who approached Abby's yellow car. "The keys are in it. Make sure the vehicle is returned to the Lady Abby Gregg. She helped us escape."

"Understood." The human man, over six-foot tall himself, folded his body into the driver's side as his human friend took the passenger seat. They left at once, one of the SUV's filled with both Prillon guards following behind. I wondered why for a few seconds, then realized the humans would need someone to drive them home after they dropped off Abby's car. Smart.

I stood in the circle of Tane's embrace, not wanting to move. I definitely didn't feel like talking. He seemed to anticipate my mood, for he picked me up and cradled me against his chest as he carried me to the closest SUV. Bahre opened the back door, and Tane slid inside with me on his lap.

The other Atlans split up, Bahre with us in this

vehicle—Quinn, I discovered, in the front passenger seat
—and Kai drove the other SUV with Egon as his
passenger.

Quinn glanced back over her seat at me. "Are you
okay?"

"Not really."

Her eyes were round and sad with empathy. "I'm so
sorry. We'll figure it out."

Would we? That's what I wanted to say. Instead I kept
my mouth shut, pressed my ear to Tane's chest, and
focused on the steady beat of his heart. I felt like I was on
a roller coaster with no way to get off. Bliss. Anger. Pleasure. Fear. Rage. Tenderness. Humiliation. Love. Back
and forth like I was a ping-pong ball being beaten to
death by two world-champion players.

George Gregg and Tane. Earth and the Coalition. My
head and my heart.

My head said this situation was a complete and total
disaster, that Tane was going to go to jail or, worse, get
kicked off the planet, and there was nothing I could do to
stop it.

My heart, however, stuck its head in the sand like an
ostrich and refused to accept the facts. My heart still
wanted a happily ever after with my fairy-tale prince.

12

Warden Egara was waiting for us when we arrived at Bahre's home, her gray eyes cold as ice. She wore her official Interstellar Brides Program uniform, the dark gray and burgundy suit looking as rigid and relentless as the woman who wore it. We had gathered underground, in Bahre's secure bunker, where we were certain no human recording devices could operate. We'd used Coalition tech to secure Bahre's home. The humans had nothing that could penetrate his defenses.

Any living being insane enough to try to sneak past Bahre's security team had a death wish. But Bahre's security precautions did not impress the warden. Not at the moment.

"What the hell happened, Bahre? How did you let Tane get into this mess? Do you even know what kind of political disaster this is?" Warden Egara sat opposite Bahre at the end of a long conference table. Everyone had taken a seat except the two Prillon guards at the door and Elena, who appeared to be too riled up to sit still.

"It's not his fault," Quinn piped up from where she sat on Bahre's right.

"And you." Warden Egara turned to glare at Quinn. "You're his mate. You know how hard we had to work to get permission for him to live on Earth. You two are still being watched like hawks. This could ruin years of work. Years. They could rescind his resident permit. Get you both kicked off planet. It would take a miracle for anyone else to be allowed to settle here. A goddamn miracle."

Quinn dropped her head into her hands with a groan as Bahre stared at the young woman who held so much power over our futures. The warden was not elderly. She was a female in her prime, once mated to two Prillon warriors. She was intelligent and our strongest ally on Earth. None of us wanted to upset her. But judging by the tight lines around her mouth, she was definitely upset. With good reason.

My mate paced along the edge of the room, walking in front of the dark series of security screens. They were not functioning at the moment, the black background outlining her body in perfect frames. I was attuned to her every move, every breath, and I knew her nervous energy returned bit by bit. I could see it in the arch of her back and the way she chewed at her bottom lip. The sound of her breathing was irregular, and she had placed her hand on top of her chest again, rubbing an invisible wound. I would fuck her again, and soon. She would drive herself to madness otherwise. She couldn't compartmentalize.

Shove her anxiety away. She needed release, and I was more than willing to provide an orgasm or two, whether she realized she needed them or not.

Mine. The beast agreed. Perhaps later we would find out exactly how much she enjoyed a good spanking.

"It's my fault."

Everyone froze at my mate's words.

Elena had stopped pacing and looked at each person in turn—Egara, Bahre, Kai, Egon, Velik—before settling her gaze on me. "I knew what kind of man Mr. Gregg was. I didn't want to know, but I knew. I never should have trusted him. We never should have stayed in that house, not even in my rooms. I should have insisted we leave. Go somewhere else. I should have known better."

Warden Egara's eyes narrowed as she inspected my mate. The room remained quiet for long moments until Elena spoke again.

"The sex tape is irrelevant. I'll give a few interviews saying it was staged. I won't press charges. Besides, Dominique can spin it; she's a public relations mastermind. She will turn the video into the next celebrity sex scandal." She turned to Bahre. "But if there really is video of you guys killing a human, and Mr. Gregg has his hands on it, you've got a *lot* bigger problems than me. He knows congressmen. Military people. Billionaires all over the world. He's connected. And he hates the Coalition."

Warden Egara shot to her feet. "What is she talking about?" She tilted her head to glare at Bahre, who had the good sense to look contrite.

"My apologies, Warden. Hive Trackers found Maxus and Vivian a few weeks ago. They tried to take Vivian hostage once they realized she was his mate. They killed a human male, a friend of hers, in their attempt to capture her. The incident was resolved. The human male in charge of the fight club assured us he would take care of the human side of the issue. We captured the Hive Trackers, as you know, the two Prillon warriors you transported to The Colony?"

"Yes. I agreed to help those two Prillon warriors. But you did not say anything about them killing a human."

"The matter was settled. They were under Hive control when they killed the man. We did not require Coalition assistance."

"If a bride was involved, I should have been informed."

"Of course," Bahre assured. "But Vivian was not in Interstellar Bride."

The Warden glared at Bahre, glanced at me; then her gaze settled on Elena, who stared straight back at her. "Perhaps not officially, but she was mine. As is Elena. Whether they've officially been through the processing center or not." She turned away from Elena to give each of the warlords at the table a stern glare. "Do not make the same mistake again. The human women are mine to protect. If you want mates, you will keep me in the loop. I don't care how dirty or messy it gets."

"Very well."

We all agreed with the warden that she was to be kept aware of all things involving her brides. She was notoriously protective of the human females as well as their mates. She took her job very seriously, matching Earth's women to worthy males in the Coalition Fleet. She saved lives, gave thousands of fighters hope. Of all the processing centers in the Coalition, Earth's was the most famous. The human brides had only been in the mix for a few short years but were already making impressive contributions. The queen of Viken was human. As was the mate of Prime Nial. Earth's females were adaptable and unpredictable. They had settled with mates on Rogue 5 and Everis and every planet in between. They'd been the first, and remained the *only* females willing to accept warriors from The Colony as mates.

That alone had made every human female cherished by every fighter in the fleet. Before human females, a Coalition fighter, warlord, or warrior banished to The Colony—like every male in this room had been—was doomed to a long, lonely life.

Females like Elena gave all of us hope. A reason to hang on. To keep fighting.

Elena's head snapped up, and I saw her fingers moving over her cell phone screen.

"Elena?" I asked.

She glanced up, then back down, and kept tapping out her message. "What's the address here? Abby is on her way." She looked up and our gazes locked. "Her security guy came through. She has all the video. Including the murder."

"Then we wait," Bahre said.

Quinn told Elena the address as the rest of the group milled around.

"She'll be here in fifteen minutes."

Abby made it in ten, the screeching of her tires on Bahre's driveway reaching my Hive-enhanced hearing even belowground. "She's here," I said.

Elena stirred from where she was sitting in my lap, her cheek to my chest as I stroked her long black hair.

"And she apparently drives angry, like someone else I know."

Elena managed a smile as she slid off my lap and walked to the doors. They were already opening, the Prillon guards escorting Abby into the meeting space as if attending a princess. More surprising was the fact that Dominique walked in right behind her.

Elena walked to her friends, and the three women formed a circle, their arms wrapped around one another, a flurry of questions and answers flying between them.

I did not wish to interrupt, nor, it appeared, did any of the other males. Quinn and Warden Egara had no hesitancy.

"Ladies, is everyone all right?" Warden Egara asked.

They turned as one to face her. Abby answered. "Yeah. Kind of."

"Fair enough."

Quinn moved forward, her jeans, pale blue blouse, and sandals nearly identical to Abby's attire. "I'm Quinn. Bahre is my mate. He's an Atlan, like Tane."

The females spoke to one another as I and the others waited in silence. I was quite sure the Prillon guards sent by Prime Nial to assist in the hunt for the Hive on Earth had not been in the presence of so many females since the ball. Nor had I, in the years before coming to Earth, been around a large number of human females. None of us appeared to know what would be welcomed and what might be seen as a threat by the small beauties. We did not want to frighten them. Terrified females did not make for good mate hunting. And I knew damn good and well the Prillons were looking for a female to call their own every moment of every day. As were the Atlans. We were all in the same position, warriors without surcease. Without peace. We needed these females to accept us.

We were on high alert, ready to kill to protect them... but we had no idea what to say to any of them. Not even me, to my own mate.

I looked to Bahre with a shrug. He cleared his throat. "Quinn? Ladies? Please, come in and take a seat." He indicated the long table, all the chairs empty now as Kai, Egon, and Velik had risen the moment Abby and Dominique entered the room.

Abby glanced at the table, then looked at me. "No thanks. I don't really want to sit down. I'm too stressed out, ya know?"

"Whatever pleases you."

I could not stay away from my mate for another moment, so I crossed the room and wrapped my arm around her waist. She leaned into me at once, melting into my side like she belonged there. Her soft sigh seemed to have a relaxing effect on Abby and Dominique as well, as they both took a deep breath and sighed.

"Well?" Dominique said.

"Showtime, I guess," Abby confirmed. She had a small bag draped over her elbow—a purse, the humans called them. She reached inside and pulled out two dark sticks about the length of her thumbs. "The blue one has the—sexy times—on it. The black one, supposedly, has that human murder."

"Have you watched them?" Elena asked.

Abby shrugged and dialed up the brightness on her smile. "Well, my guys are good. Turns out they actually helped Daddy make that stupid rape video, so they have all the real video they used to make the bad version already separated out. Super easy." She held out the blue stick to Elena, who took it and shoved it in the front pocket of her pants. "I didn't watch the other one, but they assured me the murder was on there."

"Let's see it." Warden Egara took the black stick and turned to face Bahre. "You do have something we can play this on, don't you?"

"Yes. But there is no need. We were all there, my lady."

"I was not there. I need to know what we're dealing with."

Kai spoke up for the first time. "Two Hive Trackers entered the fight club. It was filled with humans. They were hunting Warlord Maxus and knew that his mate, Vivian, was in the club unprotected. They entered and approached Vivian. Her friend, an elder human male, stepped in front of them to protect Vivian. The Hive executed him in order to reach her."

Warden Egara digested that for a few seconds. "And then what happened?"

"We arrived with Maxus, detained the two Hive Trackers—the Prillon warriors you helped us send to Dr. Surnen on The Colony—and sedated Maxus. The human Snook, a criminal who owns the fight club, assured us he would take care of the elder's body as well as the local authorities, as the man had also been a friend of his."

"Shit. Let me see it," the warden demanded.

Kai took the stick and walked to one of the workstations along the wall, to a desk beneath one of the dark screens. Moments later we all watched in silence as the entire sequence of events we'd survived in order to ensure Maxus and his mate were safe and together played out on the screen.

The moment the Hive Trackers eliminated the human without hesitation or remorse made both Abby and Dominique gasp. Elena's stricken face looked sad. She reached for my hand and squeezed.

"That's the Hive?" she whispered.

"Some of them. Those are the Trackers, specialists. Not their typical Soldiers. The Soldiers are usually bigger and much more cruel."

"I'm so sorry." She rested her head against my shoulder. "Humans have no idea, do we? Absolutely no idea."

"No, they do not." Warden Egara indicated with a flick of her hand at Kai that she wanted the remote control he was using to play the video. He gave it to her without comment, and she muted the video before fast-forwarding to the end.

And fuck, there was a lot of video after the human had died. Whoever had taken the video had watched and recorded everything we had done or said in that room for more than half an hour.

"How did you not know you were under surveillance?" the warden demanded.

"The video was taken by a female," Kai responded. "I caught her scent when I returned to the club to make sure we had taken care of everything properly."

That actually made the warden smile. "I have tried to tell you gentlemen, Earth women are not helpless damsels in distress. You paid no attention to the scent because you assumed no female could be a threat."

"Apparently," Bahre agreed. "Not one of us was aware of her presence."

"Vivian was," Quinn piped up. "She told me she made eye contact with her during the chaos. And if you watch the video again, you'll see when Vivian looks up into the corner of the ceiling."

Kai cleared his throat. "I have been searching for her every day since. I will find her."

Warden Egara made a strange snorting sound but didn't argue. "I'm going to call my friend in the Senate. Kai, grab that video. Ladies, stay here, where it's safe. Warlords, and Quinn, you come with me. Now. We need to nip this in the bud. Maybe we can get them to release our video first, highlight the way the Coalition warlords were protecting Earth from the evil Hive Trackers. Something like that. But we have to get our version of events out first."

She turned on her heel and walked toward the Prillon guards.

"Let's go, gentlemen. We do *not* have time to spare." She pulled her cell phone from a pocket and was already speaking as her voice disappeared down the long corridor. "Yes, Senator, it's Catherine Egara. Yes. Yes. From the Interstellar Brides Program? Yes, I'm still in Miami. Listen, I'm in a bit of a pickle..."

A pickle? What did that have to do with the dead human or a video?

"Tane." Elena was looking at the blue stick she now held in her hand. I had not seen her remove it from her pocket.

I leaned down and took her mouth in a kiss. A deep, hungry, soul-searing kiss that made my cock hard and my beast stir. "One thing at a time. Stay here. Be safe. When I return, we'll take care of Mr. Gregg and his video collection. Okay?"

She nodded but I could see the argument building behind her dark eyes.

"Please. If your people decide to stop sending brides..." I stroked her cheek with the pad of my thumb. "We need Earth, Elena. We need brides for our fighters. And I need you. Need to know you are safe so I can go take care of this."

"All right." She kissed me and stepped back. "Go get 'em."

I did not wish to leave Elena's side, but I had been part of the team that night, the night the human had died. I was there. If Warden Egara needed us to go speak to the human government to make sure Earth was still willing to send human brides to the Coalition, then I had to go. There were too many warriors who would suffer, too many warlords who would die if we did not secure our position here on Earth.

"Come here." I kissed her again and deactivated the pain actuators in her mating cuffs. Mine would send streaks of fire up my arms, remind me and my beast that we had to remain in control, that our mate needed us. I welcomed that reminder. Needed it.

Elena, however, did not need to suffer. "I'll be back as soon as I can."

"I love you, Tane."

Every cell inside my body froze as her words penetrated, sinking deep, healing parts of me I hadn't realized were broken. I pulled her close and kissed her again. And again.

Dominique cleared her throat.

Elena wrapped her hands around my neck, buried her fingers in my hair, pulled me closer.

"Tane, let's go, brother," Kai shouted to me from the corridor.

With a sigh I felt all the way to my beast's barren soul, I ended the kiss and settled my forehead against my mate's. "I love you, Elena. You are mine."

She nodded and stepped back. Everything in me wanted to remain at her side. She was my center of gravity. But I had work to do.

Fuck.

I followed Kai and the others and left my mate behind.

13

"So much alpha male energy in the room makes it hard to think." Dominique grabbed the flash drive out of my hands and walked over to the screen we'd been using to watch the murder tape.

"Those Hive are scary," Abby said. "I don't know why they don't show that kind of stuff on the news. All the anti-alien protests would go away if they did." She sat at the large conference table in the chair closest to Dominique.

Dominique held the remote and turned on the playback. "People will believe what they want to believe. Even if we showed them that video, they'd just think it was a deep fake or special effects." Seconds later I saw myself and Tane in my room. I was laid out on the standing desk, and we were going at it, kissing, touching, hands moving around like we were on fire, frantic to get at each other. Clearly Tane and I were about to fuck like a couple of wild animals. My body heated as the memory of exactly what each of those touches, those kisses had felt like.

"Don't play that," I said.

Dominique shooed at me with her hand. "I already watched this with Abby earlier."

"You did?" God, could I be more embarrassed?

"Don't worry. And Abby's security friend wasn't kidding. They cherry-picked the scenes they wanted to use. All you have to do is get this to go viral. Give an interview about how you are releasing the 'real sex tape.'" She made air quotes with her fingers. "And then play up the Cinderella angle, say someone is so jealous of you that they are trying to ruin your happily-ever-after, hot-sex, Prince Charming life."

"One, who's going to believe me? I'm literally a nobody. I don't even have a social media profile. Anywhere." I hated all of it. The only people I wanted to communicate with had my cell phone number. They could send me a damn text message.

"Who cares?" Abby asked. "All you have to do is cast doubt on Daddy's version. And trust me, when they see you begging Tane to—uh…" She glanced up from picking at her manicure to meet my gaze. "Well, let's just say, it's sexy. It's totally believable. And when they play the two videos side by side, it will be totally obvious that the sounds were stolen and put in the wrong places."

"And," Dominique added, "you are *Cinderella*, girlfriend. You got the beast at the ball, your very own Prince Charming. Trust me, *everyone* wants to see you two getting it on. *And* he's an alien? Who doesn't want to know what an alien's junk looks like? You'll go viral so fast your head will spin."

I hated every word my friends said, and they were one hundred percent right. Tane was off taking care of a real problem, one that could result in all the Interstellar Brides Processing Centers being closed. Permanently. I could deal with this. Right? Stupid sex tape. Piece of cake. Embarrassing. Humiliating. Non-lethal. Piece of damn cake.

"Okay. Fine. But who do we know that can launch this kind of sex video anyway?" I looked at Abby. "I know you have a lot of followers, but not enough. Not for this. And you're my friend. No credibility. We need the video to go viral so fast Mr. Gregg doesn't know what hit him."

Dominique stopped the video and removed the flash drive. "I happen to have the perfect idea. The solution of all solutions to this problem." Her tone of voice was way too satisfied. Whatever she had in mind, I was going to hate it.

Oh God. "You're actually terrifying, you know that?"

She waggled her eyebrows at me. "Let's go."

I looked down at my thrown-together pants and shirt, fretted for a second over my lack of panties, dismissed that one, and stared at my friend. "I look like hell. I can't go anywhere like this."

"Oh yes, you can. Trust me. You'll look like a super-model by the time we get you on-screen."

———

"Ladies, come in. Come in."

I took two steps backward and bumped into Abby,

who had been coming up the stairs right behind me. "No way. This is so not a good idea."

Dominique smiled her best fake smile at Chet Bosworth, ridiculous hair, oversize teeth, drama king announcer of the *Bachelor Beast* television show, and reached behind her, blindly flailing around for me until I relented and placed my hand in hers.

Shit. This was such a bad idea. Worse, I couldn't think of a better one.

The two Prillon warriors who had accompanied us didn't say a word, but they did give Chet a thorough inspection that had the man practically jumping out of his skin with nerves. "Oh my. Prillon warriors. To what do I owe the honor?"

"We are here to protect the females." This Prillon warrior assigned to guard us was named Krag. He was big, like all of them, but his skin was dark like the stained walnut desk in Mr. Gregg's office. The other Prillon, standing guard behind Abby on the rock stairs leading to Chet's front door, was a color I had not seen before. Golden like the metal, but not shiny. Much darker than the light gold of the Prillon guard at the ball, and nothing at all like the copper-colored guard we'd met that night, either.

I wondered how many different skin tones the Prillons had, wondered if they were like humans and had preconceived ideas about their warriors based on their color. I hoped not. If advanced aliens were still fighting over race, was there any hope at all for humanity to get their act together?

"I will inspect your home now." Krag spoke to Chet

and then walked past the human man, whose mouth was opening and closing with no words coming out.

Dominique patted Chet on the shoulder and followed Krag inside Chet's home. I followed with a shrug. "They are very particular about making sure we're safe."

"I see that." He spoke to me, but he was staring at the golden warrior coming up the stairs. "I didn't get a chance to see any of you Prillons up close at the ball."

"There is nothing to see." The golden warrior, Rohn, ushered us inside and stopped, watching Chet. "You are also under our protection, sir. Please go inside."

Chet seemed truly gobsmacked.

Abby laughed. "Chet Bosworth with nothing to say. I didn't know that was possible."

"Very funny, girl." He walked into his own house, stopped in the foyer, and then held out his hand to Dominique. "All right, let's see it."

Dominique placed the blue flash drive into Chet's open palm. "The real video feed is first. Fast-forward and you will find the bad one."

"By bad I assume you mean the video of an Atlan warlord, a star from *my show*, committing sexual assault?" He sounded disgusted. "Trust me, I've seen it already."

I wanted to sink into the floor and die.

"Bad for ratings?" Abby asked.

"Terrible. They want to cancel the show. Can you believe that? The president of the network called me this afternoon, threatened to sue me. *Me!* Unbelievable. After all the work I put into those beasts. The network is run by a bunch of rat bastards, the lot of them." Chet walked through the well lit hallway to a bright, cheery kitchen decorated with sunflowers. There he moved to the table and sat. We joined him and waited as he plugged the flash drive into his laptop, put on his headphones, and sat back to watch.

A few minutes later he removed the headphones and looked at me. "This is pure gold. We stream this live, no taping, no way for them to know what we're going to do or say. Got that?"

"Okay. But what am I going to say?"

Chet picked up his cell phone. "You leave that to me. I'll draw up some talking points." He had gone from irritated to almost giddy. "This is so good. God, they're going to beg me to do another season. Beg me." He pushed his call button and looked at me. "I'm going to charge them double. Low-life scum, threaten to take me to court."

"I'll help with the talking points. Don't worry." Dominique reached for my hand, and I immediately felt better. Chet Bosworth seemed like a decent enough man now that I had been in his home. The place was comfortable, filled with warm colors and soft lighting. A place to relax, not impress others. His hair wasn't spiked up from his head like a porcupine's quills, and he wasn't trying to sell anything. In jeans, a T-shirt, bare feet, and sloppy hair he'd obviously done little more than finger comb after a shower, he seemed almost...human.

I heard a feminine voice through his phone.

"Julia, darling, it's me. This is a 9-1-1 call. Top secret. I need you over here ASAP."

He listened as the woman replied.

"My place. Yes. Now. Like, *an hour ago* now. I've got two ladies and myself for makeup and hair. We've got to look like a million dollars. And I need you to talk Tony into bringing over his camera. The good one, not that piece of shit with the smudged lens."

More questions.

"No no no. I know it's not on the schedule. Tell him it's a matter of national security."

Pause.

"Yes, I did just say that. And Julia, you and Tony. No one else. I mean it. Don't tell anyone. This is big, dear. Really, really big." Chet was smiling now. "I promise I'll make it worth your time." He laughed. "Trust me, you don't want to miss it."

————

SEVERAL HOURS later Abby and I were seated across from Chet Bosworth, television *personality,* in a small studio in his basement. The chairs were covered in beige fabric and looked like they belonged in a fairy-tale castle. The backdrop I could just make out behind us on the monitor *looked* like a set of large bay windows. If you believed the screen, we were sitting in front of those windows over-looking a garden. In reality we were in front of a green screen, a giant sheet of green paper attached to the wall from floor to ceiling. The rest was computer magic.

Tony had brought the *good camera.*

Julia had turned Dominique into an absolute queen just in case she needed to go in front of the camera. Abby looked young and innocent. Pale pink lips. All natural makeup. Her once-platinum-blonde hair was now a soft, natural color more like caramel. She was going to play the part of the scandalized, helpless billionaire's daughter who had been protected and shielded from the naughty side of life. That wouldn't jive with her current social media platform, but her brand had focused mainly on fashion, makeup, and shoes. She had a lot of room to grow her audience.

And me? I didn't look half bad, if I did say so myself. I didn't appear to be the kind of woman who would make a sex tape, but I didn't look like a nobody with a teaching degree either. My makeup was subtle but made my eyes seem to be bigger than I'd ever seen them, dark and mysterious. I had changed into a sleek burgundy pants suit with matching heels and a pale pink blouse that was almost white. I presented as professional and soft. Feminine and earnest. My hair was up in a loose bun with tendrils framing my face, the burgundy lipstick I wore just dark enough to draw attention but not appear to be trying too hard. The mating cuffs I wore were discreetly hidden under the suit jacket's sleeves, ready to be revealed at the appropriate moment.

I looked rich. I had that polished persona that wealthy people acquire through years of professional hair, clothing, and makeup. Julia had even done my nails, giving them a demure set of pink nails tipped in white. Nothing about me was unpolished, aggressive, or threatening in any way.

I could be a lifestyle magazine model. Or a *baking* celebrity. Or a social media personality who focused on raising money for something completely noncontroversial, like a children's hospital or no-kill animal shelters. Puppies and kittens and kids. Who didn't love 'em?

Chet settled into the third chair facing us, exactly like the two Abby and I were sitting in, and arranged his clothing.

"You look like a peacock," Abby said. "I love that color."

"Thank you, dear. I love this one myself. But I still think it might have been a mistake not to go with the dramatic red and black." His attire consisted of a pair of shiny teal-blue pants, a matching jacket with tails that fell to below his knees in back, a matching vest lined with pearl buttons, and a soft purple dress shirt under it all. His blond, spiked, and shined hair was set off by the yellow in his necktie, which was tucked neatly into the vest, showing barely more than a hand's width of dark purple, teal, and golden designs embroidered to look like peacock feathers.

Even his socks matched, light purple tucked into dark brown shoes.

He was serious about the black outfit. Abby and I looked at one another and grinned.

"No. The black is too somber. You'd look like you were trying to be a vampire," Abby assured him.

"Oh, no no no. I don't do goth." He slipped a pair of false veneers into his mouth, and I realized I was just now seeing the television version of Chet. Real Chet looked like he shopped at the farmers' market on the weekend and enjoyed quiet music and a nice glass of wine. He smoothed his tongue over his new, much whiter, much larger front teeth and practiced his huge, very dramatic smile on both of us. "Well, ladies, how do I look? This thing's going to go viral. I need to make the most of it."

"You're asking the wrong person," I said.

Abby, however, tilted her head and considered his question much more seriously. "You need more pink on your lips and a bit more blush. That teal is making you look washed out under these lights." She pointed to the monitor where we could see what the set looked like on camera. "And I'm not feeling the whole garden vibe. That's too British for Miami. We're talking about a sex tape, not having afternoon tea."

Chet steepled his fingers and looked at Abby with new appreciation. "Very right. About everything." He snapped his fingers. "Julia? Darling? I need more color." He looked at the cameraman. "Tony, what else have we got for backdrops?"

"What do you want, boss?"

Chet looked at Abby. "Why don't you choose something, my dear?"

Abby hopped to her feet and joined Tony, the two discussing the options for our false surroundings as I leaned back in my chair and waited. My hand instinctively wrapped around my locket, and I wondered what my mother would think of this mess. Or my grandmother?

Father Joseph? He'd been gone for a few years now, but he'd always been kind to me when I was a child at Sunday mass. He would probably be appalled.

Hell, I was appalled and I hadn't done anything but enjoy Tane's attention. Sure, more than once. And we weren't legally married. Sin. Sin. Sin. But it wasn't like I was an entirely different person just because some asshole decided to ruin my life with a fake video. Or because I'd fallen in love with an alien.

There it was again. That word. *Love.* I was in love with Tane. Totally. Completely. Ready to leave this stupid planet, in love with him. Yet I had no idea where he was right now. What he was doing. Who he was talking to. Important people, no doubt.

I was sitting here watching Chet Bosworth have deep red rouge applied to his already dark cheeks. The man wore enough stage makeup to support an entire shopping center single-handedly. Truly he was barely recognizable as the man who had answered the door a few hours earlier.

"You're a good-looking man, you know. You don't need all that." I tapped my fingertips on the curved arms of the interview chair. "You should just be yourself."

Chet laughed, but the sound was sad, not amused. "Oh my dear, if only that were true." Julia finished with his lips, and he leaned forward to wink at me. "No one wants to listen to a thirtysomething gay man from Nebraska named Charles Milner talk about anything. Trust me."

Abby appeared to be pleased with herself as she plopped back down into the chair next to me. Her outfit consisted of a cream-colored top, pale jeans, sandals, and a heart pendant on loan from Julia because they agreed it made her look younger and more sympathetic. "You might be surprised, Charlie."

"Chet."

"Charlie." Abby smacked her glossy pink lips and winked at me. "Charlie Milner from Nee-brasss-kuh. Check it out." She pointed at the monitor where a new image appeared on the screen behind us.

I squinted, my contacts still not in my eyes and my distance vision still sucking. Was that Tane? Naked?

Dominique chuckled. "Go big or go home, I guess."

"Damn right about that," Chet agreed. "Nice ass on that one."

Abby crossed her arms. "Tony, you got that sex tape ready to roll?"

"Yes, ma'am."

She looked up at me. "Let's do this."

Yes, let's go in front of millions of people and talk about my feelings for Tane and our hot sex and how I was so desperate to have an orgasm I had been sobbing, begging an alien beast to fuck me harder. All while staring at a picture of him from the back. The naked, rock-hard, perfect-ass back.

I looked at Abby. "Is that really necessary?" Tane's bare backside and a nice bit of his muscled back, a red rectangular sign stamped over the top that read "ALIEN SEX TAPE" in huge, red block letters.

"Oh yeah. Total clickbait. Tane has a really nice ass."

Thank God my mother was dead. This would have killed her.

14

ane, Underground Military Base somewhere in Florida

I SAT NEXT to Warlord Bahre. Quinn was on his other side, and Warden Egara was on mine. Seated across from us were three very unhappy humans. One vice admiral. One colonel. And one woman in a suit who wore no insignia but did most of the talking.

Apparently she and Warden Egara knew one another.

"The video from the fight club has already been distributed to the appropriate committee members in congress as well as select members of the military and intelligence community."

Warden Egara leaned forward, her forearms on top of the dark table. "That was a mistake. We are having enough difficulty maintaining political and military support for the Coalition as it is. This is not going to help.

The human did die, and that is a tragedy, but he was killed by Hive Trackers, not my warlords."

"Hive Trackers sent to hunt one of your warlords, Warden. An Atlan who, as I understand it, arrived with a Hive reconnaissance team, killed the other members of that team, and then set up on Earth, playing house with no one the wiser."

Fuck. I leaned back until my shoulders hit the high-backed chair. The humans knew about Maxus and Vivian. Knew that Maxus had been living on Earth. That he broke both Coalition and human law.

"We neutralized the problem," I said. "Maxus has been removed to Atlan."

"We should have been informed immediately," the general said. "You people keep withholding information and then wonder why our leaders don't trust you. This is exactly why we can't get approval for more Coalition forces to be stationed here on Earth." He was in his fifties, with a hard look in his eyes I recognized in a fellow fighter. He had scars on his soul, just like we did.

Bahre tilted his chin toward the general and took Quinn's hand in his, making them a united front. "You are correct. We should have told your people about the civilian death. We did warn you about the increased Hive presence on your planet. And your leaders did nothing. If knowledge of this man's death reached the public, it could cause panic or overreaction."

"And why would we panic, warlord?" the woman asked. She stood up and placed her hands on the table, leaning forward in an aggressive stance. She had balls of steel facing down an Atlan warlord like that. "A human was killed. Tragic, but it happens every day, thousands of times. What concerns us, my friends, is the fact that there appears to be significant Hive activity on *our planet.* Part of our agreement with the Coalition of Planets was that you would provide protection for Earth generally, and from the Hive specifically. *That* is why Earth continues to send fighters and brides to you people. And it would seem you are not keeping your part of the bargain."

"If I may..." Warden Egara began.

"You may not." The woman looked at me, then Bahre. "Are either one of you authorized to speak for the Coalition?"

Fuck. I was not. Not even close. I was an outcast banished to The Colony. I did not and could not begin to imagine what Prime Nial, the leader of the Prillon people and basically their king, would or would not agree to. But he did have personal interest in Earth, as his bride was human. His daughter was half-human. And she would care about what was happening on Earth. A lot.

"Prime Nial's mate is from Earth. As is the queen of Viken. We have human brides mated to battleship commanders and fighters alike. Earth is very important to the Coalition, I assure you." Warden Egara was tapping her fingernails on top of the table in a repeating rhythm. "Let's cut the crap, Jennifer. What does your boss want?"

Jennifer, the human female, grinned and raised a brow at the warden. "Catherine, I knew there was a reason we were friends."

"Well?"

Jennifer looked at the general, who nodded his approval, then the colonel, who dipped his chin as well.

"We want the truth. How many Coalition warriors are

here? How many Hive? We want technology that can track them as well as weapons that can eliminate them."

"Shoot a fucking bullet at these things and they don't even slow down," the colonel sounded angry. "I'm losing good soldiers."

"Where?" Bahre asked.

"You first," Jennifer said. She was young and beautiful, her body lithe and curved behind a dark brown pair of pants and matching jacket. Her shirt was white, the contrast making her curly light brown hair appear to be a halo around her head. "How many? Where are they? What kind of invasion force are we dealing with? And when?"

Warden Egara cleared her throat. "We have no idea."

"Bullshit," the general said.

Bahre confirmed the warden's words. "She is telling you the truth. We were unaware of the Hive Trackers until the incident with Maxus. We had no idea the Hive were sending reconnaissance teams to Earth. The Hive have taken a marked interest in human females out in Coalition Space. Several kidnap attempts have been made. We also recently discovered a secret facility where the Hive were attempting to impregnate human women."

"How many women?" Jennifer's voice had gone low and sinister. I had a feeling the woman was much more dangerous than she looked.

"A couple dozen. They'd been kidnapped from Earth."

"Fucking hell." The colonel leaned back in his chair. "Well? Weapons? Soldiers? We'll take care of the video; our asset acquired it. We can spin that any way we need to. Focus on the Hive threat. We can use it to get a budget increase, but we need a plan."

"Your asset acquired the video? One of your people?" I asked.

"Yes," Jennifer said and looked at me, dead in the eye.

Oh fuck. Was Kai hunting for a human spy? Was he hunting for Jennifer?

"Unlike the sex tape." She looked at me. "I blame you for that one, *Prince Charming*. That sloppy bastard nailed you in your mate's private quarters. What were you thinking? You should have checked for surveillance more than once."

Shame flooded my entire body, made me feel like I was too heavy to stand up, even if I was ready to leave my chair. "I take full responsibility. Once we are finished here, I will deal with that problem."

Jennifer looked confused. "It's already been handled, brilliantly, I might add."

"What are you talking about?"

Jennifer ran her hands over the top of the desk, and some screens I hadn't paid attention to turned on, their contents clearly visible through the glass. With a grin I was sure meant I was *not* going to like what I saw next, she scrolled past several menus, selected what she wanted, and...

"Can we say Alien Sex Tape? People, you've all seen the other one, that horrible video that made it appear as if our warlord, our *Beast Charming committed a heinous act of betrayal against his chosen bride."* Chet fucking Bosworth was sitting in a bright teal suit smiling at my mate like they were best friends. And Elena? Fuck. She looked

amazing. Kissable. Fuckable. So feminine and sweet. And behind them on a large screen?

"Holy shit." Quinn burst out laughing, then quickly covered her mistake with a hand over her mouth.

Bahre squinted, then rumbled, the growl one of displeasure.

I had no idea why *they* were reacting so strongly. It was *my ass* on that screen. And my back, most of it. They'd slapped some type of graphic over my ass cheeks —*almost*—hiding everything. The lines and scars from my time with the Hive were there, unaltered and on display. There would be no doubt that was me.

I leaned over the table and took a closer look. Was that Elena's leg wrapped around my hip?

"What the fuck?" I stood up so I could get a better, more direct view as the insanity continued.

"I'm here to tell you, I am sitting in my studio with Cinderella herself, Miss Elena Garcia. She lives right here in Florida, folks. And she's with me today to set the record straight the only way she can—" Chet leaned toward the camera, his huge front teeth gleaming, the edge of his hand on one side of his mouth so anyone watching would know what he was about to tell them was a secret. *"She gave us the* real, unedited *tape. Ladies, if you want to know the hot, sexy, dirty details of what it's like to be claimed by an Atlan warlord, do not move a muscle!"*

Chet settled back in his chair, and the camera angle pulled away to show Chet and both of his guests. Not just Elena. Abby was there.

Her father was going to be furious. Brave young lady.

"So, Elena, what's it like to be mated to a beast?"

I groaned and slapped my hand over my face. Jennifer

was smiling at me. Warden Egara looked thoughtful. The general and the colonel had moved to a corner of the room to have a private discussion. Apparently they were unaware of the fact that both Bahre and I had Hive-enhanced hearing. We heard every word. Nothing surprising was said. Operational details. Weapons. Logistics of having more aliens on Earth. The budget they were going to ask for. Mundane, save-the-planet kinds of things.

My *mate* was discussing what it was like to fuck me, and I could not turn away.

Chet started the video, pausing dramatically at the most revealing moments, seconds before Elena would cry out with her orgasm, or just after I'd told her what I was going to do to her body next.

Oh yes, Elena, the whole world needs to know exactly what you were feeling every moment I had my cock or tongue or fingers on or inside your body.

I suspected a human male would have been ashamed at such exposure. My beast and I, however, preened with every word from Elena's mouth. She told the other humans watching that I was an *amazing lover.* That she'd never experienced pleasure like she had with me, or as many orgasms. Not only had my mate accepted me, found me worthy, but she was broadcasting to the world her unconditional love and praise for me as her mate.

No warlord would ever dare dream of such pride from a mate. Prime Nial and his second, Ander, perhaps knew how filled with pride I was. Their mate had accepted their claiming on a live comm broadcast to the entire Coalition of Planets after Nial had challenged for leadership in a fighting arena on Prillon Prime

The arena had been full of spectators.

She had fucked her mates freely, eagerly, in front of the universe. Had welcomed a scarred, integrated Prillon warrior who had been banished to The Colony and actually been denied a mate.

This kind of acceptance, love, changed things for everyone. And this time it was me. My mate. My mating cuffs around her wrists.

I watched the entire interview. Every moment of our bodies entwined made me miss her more. Pain shot up my arms every few seconds, a reminder that Elena was mine. That beautiful, courageous, amazing female was mine.

My cock grew hard under the table. I'd show her amazing orgasms.

"Oh my God, this is going to change everything." Quinn had her fingers intertwined, her chin resting on both hands as she watched the video.

Bahre rose to join Warden Egara, Jennifer, the general, and the colonel as Quinn and I watched the rest of the video. I was...entranced. I could not look away.

When it was over, Quinn whistled, a sound I'd never heard her make before. "Oh my God, they posted that video less than an hour ago and it already has over ten million views."

"Is that a lot?"

She nodded and looked at me. "This is huge. I've got to get you and Elena on my segment before you two leave. But you should probably give Chet an exclusive first. He just saved your ass."

"Leave?"

She looked at me like my wits were muddled. Perhaps

they were. All I could think about was getting to my mate, taking her clothes off, and fucking her. Tasting her. Kissing her. Thanking her for the gift she had just given me.

My eyes felt like they were burning.

Quinn took one look at me and patted me on the shoulder. "I totally get it. She loves you, Tane. Like end-of-the-world, go-with-you-to-another-planet love. Congratulations."

Tears burned. Slipped from my eyes to slide down my cheeks.

Fuck. I had not expected this kind of love. Passion. Lust. Need. A mate who would allow me the honor of protecting her, providing for her comfort and her pleasure. But I had not dared hope for a female's heart to belong to me. I was not worthy. I was contaminated. Captured. Weak. I had failed her already, allowing the video to be taken in the first place.

And yet my Elena chose me. Fought for me. Shouted her love and need of me to her entire planet. And she had. She'd sat in a chair opposite Chet Bosworth and said she loved me. That she couldn't wait to start her new life with me on The Colony.

By the gods, my heart hurt so badly I was afraid the damn thing was being ripped to pieces inside my chest.

Was love supposed to hurt like this? I rubbed my chest and asked Quinn quietly.

She covered my hand with hers, her gaze soft. "Yes. When it's real, it hurts like hell."

I wiped another drop of burning liquid from my cheek and regained my senses as Bahre gave the three humans a rundown on the additional Prillon warriors and Atlan warlords Prime Nial had ordered to Earth to protect the processing centers.

Warden Egara pulled a comm unit from her purse and sent a direct call to Prillon Prime. Prime Nial himself answered.

"Warden Egara, my second favorite human. How can I be of service?"

"Hi!" A lovely woman waved at the warden from behind her mate.

"Hello, Jessica. Are you well?"

"Everything's great. How are you? You sending me a new friend? We need more human girls out here on Prillon Prime."

"I will see what I can do."

Jessica laughed. "No, you won't. The computer match is the perfect match."

Warden Egara smiled and inclined her head. "Indeed it is."

"I can't argue with that." Jessica disappeared from view, and Prime Nial's face filled the handheld comm screen.

"How can I be of assistance, Warden?"

The group of humans spoke to Prime Nial, Earth's representatives getting what they wanted—access to the leader of the Coalition Fleet without the interference of their politicians. The general said as much. Prime Nial agreed, politics made things more difficult.

I paced. I didn't give a fuck what they decided to do. How many warriors were sent to Earth or when or where they would stay. Did. Not. Care. I needed my mate. Needed to feel her against me, know she was real.

Because right now she felt like a dream that was too good to be true.

I looked at the mating cuffs on my wrists.

Real. Fucking real.

I closed my eyes and counted every second I was away from my Elena. My mate.

My heart.

15

THE TWO PRILLON WARRIORS, Krag and Rohn, escorted not only me but two additional ladies to Bahre's home. More like secure alien military base. Sheesh. I didn't have any idea what time it was. It was dark, that was all I knew. And I missed Tane.

As we pulled up to the gate, I noticed even more guards patrolling the perimeter. The gate guard, a huge Atlan I did not recognize, waved us through, and we pulled up in front of the mansion.

Abby and Dominique had spent the entire car ride analyzing every word I'd said during my interview with Chet. The video. The millions of views—and climbing—that the video was receiving online.

I was a worldwide viral sensation. The rape tape had been huge, but an *unedited* sex tape with an alien from the *Bachelor Beast* television show? And not just any beast, but Warlord Tane, the star of the Cinderella-style match-making ball?

"Oh my God, yes!" Dominique fist pumped the air. "We just got picked up by the networks."

Abby's eyes grew round. "Holy shit. Elena, you are going to be literally everywhere. There won't be a scientist in Antarctica that doesn't know about you and Tane and that video."

"Great." Shit. What had I done? Had I made a mistake?

No. No mistake. Tane was innocent. The Atlans were honorable. They deserved to be defended when someone —namely Mr. George Gregg and friends—told a lie about them. Tane was wonderful.

I rubbed the mating cuffs around my wrists as the door opened. Krag stood there. Instead of stepping back to allow me to exit the vehicle, he blocked me in, and his gaze sought mine.

"What you did today, my lady, will give hope and peace to many warriors. Coalition fighters are deemed less, unworthy, once they have been captured by the Hive. We are contaminated. No females from our own worlds would accept us."

"I'm sorry." That sounded terrible. I knew, from the little I'd spoken about the issue with Tane and from watching the *Bachelor Beast* television show, that the guys on The Colony had a bad time of it. But I had no idea that literally no other women—alien females—in the entire universe would take one of these guys as a mate. That was stupid. "Those females are clearly idiots."

"I agree." Dominique's face appeared over my shoulder, and she looked up at Krag. "You guys are gorgeous."

Krag bowed at the waist and stepped back so I could finally get out of the damn SUV. "I wanted you to know, my lady, to understand. Tane has now been elevated among all Atlan warlords. He will be the beast all others compare themselves to."

My feet hit cobblestone. "Why?"

"A warlord is only deemed worthy if a female accepts him as a mate."

"That's stupid." Here I was repeating myself.

"That is their way. It is also the Prillon way, but the Atlans are even more vehement in their belief. A worthy warlord will be chosen, accepted, and mated."

"Well, I guess the others will think Tane is worthy then, yeah? Instead of a criminal? That's good, right?" I glanced over my shoulder at Dominique and now Abby, who was climbing down right behind her.

Krag shook his head and dropped to one knee before me. "You honor us all, my lady. Before every living soul on your world, you defended your mate, chose him, honored him. No female from our worlds has ever done such a thing."

"It's no big deal. We had to—" The words died in my throat as the house and grounds emptied of warriors and warlords, fighters and I don't know what kind of aliens. Every one of them gathered around and knelt before me like I was a queen.

The silence creeped into my blood, my bones, as frogs and crickets sang to all of us.

Behind me, Abby whispered quietly, "Holy shit, Elena."

I looked over my shoulder from Abby's face to Dominique's. The silence stretched. The aliens remained kneeling. Tears seemed to be having a party on my face, because I couldn't stop them from rolling down my cheeks. "What am I supposed to do?" I whispered.

Dominique and Abby both shrugged.

I turned around to Krag and Rohn and the dozens of kneeling aliens spread out behind them. "Thank you. You guys can get up now. Okay?"

Krag shook his head. "We await the arrival of your mate. He is at the gate."

"Tane?" Yes! He was here.

As if on cue, another SUV rolled to a stop directly behind the vehicle we stood beside. The door was opening and Tane was on the ground, running, before the wheels stopped rolling. "Elena."

I ran to him and leaped into his arms. He swung me around, and everything was right in the world. My tears were happy now, my relief at being with him so powerful I felt dizzy, like I was literally going to faint.

"Tane! Is everything okay? Did you take care of the murder tape?"

"All is well, mate." He stopped spinning, kissed me once on the lips, hard and fast, and then set me on my feet. As the others had done, he dropped to one knee before me.

"Tane, what are you doing?"

"I am not worthy of you, Elena. You honor me. I am proud to be yours."

Behind him, Bahre appeared from the driver's side and joined his friend a few steps away. Kneeling. For me. Me. I was a big fat nobody from nowhere. An orphan of immigrant parents. A girl with a teaching degree and no students.

This man, alien, mate was too good to be true. But I didn't care. I was keeping him. On Earth. On his planet. On The Colony. Didn't matter to me as long as I was with him.

"I love you, Tane. Please get up."

"You spoke to Chet Bosworth. Shared your pleasure, the pleasure I gave you, with your entire world. I can never repay you for such an honor."

"About that." I placed my palm against Tane's cheek. "Chet did have one little tiny condition..."

"Anything, mate."

"We have to get married, Cinderella style, huge dress, you dressed up like a prince, all the trimmings. And we have to do it live on *Bachelor Beast*."

I didn't know what I expected, but it was not for Tane to throw back his head and laugh.

I leaned forward, for he was nearly my height, even kneeling, and kissed him.

His beast took over. With a roar he lifted me over his shoulder and carried me into the house.

————

Tane

MINE.

I had to kiss her. Touch her. Taste her. Claim her.

Mine.

My mate had sacrificed everything for me. Her

privacy. Her reputation. Her social standing. Her job. Her life on Earth. Everything. My mind wandered to the engraving on her locket. I did not know who this John had been, but he seemed to be wise.

"Greater love hath no man than this: that a man lay down his life for his friends."

I wasn't her friend, not in that sense, but I was hers. And she had proven that she would do anything, sacrifice anything, to protect me. For a warlord like me, contaminated, scarred, forsaken by my own people, she was literally a miracle.

The beast was in a rage to reach her, so I stopped fighting him and let him out.

With a growl of impatience, he lifted Elena over our shoulder and carried her past the kneeling warriors and warlords. They honored my female, as they should. She was worthy.

I reached my rooms at Bahre's compound quickly. I slammed the door. No need to bother with a lock; no male here would be foolish enough to enter without permission if he wished to keep his head attached to his body.

"Tane, put me down."

"No. Mine." The beast had thought about what he would do once we had Elena here, in our room. There was a place in this room for a beast to claim his mate properly, and I carried her to the small sitting shelf and sat her soft bottom down.

"Want you. Fuck now."

Elena's laughter was like a soothing balm on the beast's fire. "Okay, you big baby. Come here." She wrapped her arms around my neck and kissed me. The beast. Us.

"Arms up." I moved slowly, deliberately making her wonder what I had in mind as I took both of her wrists in one hand and lifted them to the wall over her head. At once the special magnetics activated, locking her mating cuffs in place, holding her hands above her head. Helpless. Trusting.

Mine.

The scent of her pussy sent mating fever rushing through my blood. The joy of not being forced to fight it made the beast roar as he lifted a hand to Elena's chest and ripped the thin blouse. The bra was beautiful. Lace. The beast liked the bra. Instead of tearing, he lifted Elena's breasts so that they were out of the contraption, lying on top like an offering. Holding her steady, he pulled her shoes off, followed by her pants until she was like a piece of art, her jacket on either side of her naked body serving as if a frame around a painting.

"Tane." She watched me now, her gaze dark and greedy as I undressed for her. She liked to look at me, and my cock got harder every moment her gaze lingered. "God, you're hot."

She was the thing that made me burn.

Dropping to my knees, I feasted on her pussy, licking and sucking until she screamed my name. I worked two fingers inside her, fucked her with them as I kissed her mouth and her breasts, sucking on her nipples, pulling them into my mouth and rolling the taut pebble over my tongue until she gasped. Until her pussy clenched around my fingers. Until I knew she was on the edge of another release.

Then I kissed her mouth.

"Tease. You are a big tease," she accused when I allowed her to take a breath.

"Mine." My beast stepped forward, kissing her as he —we—filled her with our cock.

Home. Bliss. Fucking heat.

Elena moaned into my mouth, and I fucked her then. The beast took her first, his seed coating the walls of her pussy, running down her thighs. But I did not relent, did not stop. I stroked her clit until she cried out, until her pussy went into spasms around my cock, and then I changed and I fucked her again as the Atlan male, the warlord who would worship and adore this female until the day I died. Love her. Need her.

I kissed her because my soul needed the connection. I held her hands in mine as I moved in and out of her pussy in slow, languorous strokes. There was no rush. I wanted to live in this moment for as long as I could. The beast would rise again soon. He needed her too. Our mate.

"I love you, Elena. I love you. I'm yours."

Elena cried out at my words, the walls of her pussy rippling in response to my vow.

Which was perfect. Fucking perfect.

My mate was fucking perfect.

Mine.

lena, One Month Later

OUR WEDDING WAS *the* event of the year. Even bigger than the ball had been. Chet was beside himself, having become a celebrity among the celebrities. He was making the rounds, doing talk shows and promoting our wedding day like it was a world championship soccer match or the Olympics.

Except, honestly, this felt bigger.

The sex tape had over a hundred million views, and kept growing. I didn't care. Tane and I were getting married, and then we were out of here, off this rock. Moving to The Colony.

"He is not going to survive the ceremony. You look so beautiful. He's going to lose it, I'm telling you. The beast is going to take over." Abby wore a dark green gown. Dominique, once more, was in her favorite dark blue.

Their jewel-toned bridesmaids' gowns were custom, expensive, and they were being paid—*being paid by the designer*—to wear them.

I laughed. "He'd better not. We made a deal with Chet. Besides, I do not want to waste this dress."

Unlike my previous ball gown, this one had been custom-made for me by one of the hottest designers in the world. No puffy tulle this time around. I stood in the center of a hand-embroidered masterpiece in ivory. The bodice hugged my body in soft cream. The designer had taken the intricate curves and style of Tane's mating cuffs and sewn the patterns into the gown in a mix of gold and silver with touches of a darker color for contrast at my waist and around the hem. The skirt was in three layers, the main, slim skirt front and center with a gorgeous overlay on either hip. I really did look like a fairy-tale princess, complete with a small tiara of real diamonds...a gift from Chet.

The gown was new, as was the tiara. Abby had given me a blue sapphire ankle bracelet to wear under the dress for my "something blue." The locket around my neck was old and precious, and the assurance I needed that somewhere out there in the universe, my family was looking down on me and giving me their blessing. How could they not? Tane was...amazing.

"Knock, knock, ladies!" Chet sashayed into the room and his jaw dropped. "Oh my God. Stunning. Unbelievable." He walked forward and gave me a kiss on the cheek. "Are you ready, my dear?"

"Yes."

"Let's roll, Charlie." Abby grabbed the bouquet with matching emerald tones and headed for the door.

"I told you not to call me that," Chet protested, but his smile was genuine. Not a *Chet Bosworth* smile. A real one.

"Don't worry, I won't tell anyone there's a real, live human under there."

"Thank you. That would be a disaster, wouldn't it?" Chet cleared his throat and adjusted his own royal-looking jacket. His outfit was a dark pewter gray, but the pattern sewn into the jacket had been done in the same pattern I wore, in black and gray. He looked incredible. Which was good, because he was about to walk me down the aisle in front of millions, maybe even billions of live television viewers.

Warden Egara had informed me that the wedding was going to be broadcast throughout the Coalition Fleet as well.

I should have been nervous. Edgy. Nauseous. Barely able to cope. But all I could think about was Tane and how happy he made me. How much I loved him. How incredible he was. I was steady as could be. Calm even. Content.

Happy. I was happy.

Dominique picked up her matching bouquet and followed Abby out the door. Our friendly Prillon guards were waiting in the corridor when I walked out on Chet's arm. They, too, were dressed for the occasion.

"Krag. Rohn. You both look amazing," Chet offered as he led me past them. They remained silent but fell into step behind us, not leaving me unprotected for a single moment.

The music was playing. I looked at Chet and gave him a kiss on the cheek. "Let's do this."

"I am honored." With a flourish of Chet's hand toward

the double doors, the two Atlans standing guard opened them to reveal a cavernous space filled top to bottom with people. Thousands of people.

Abby went out first, looking fabulous. Her father, Mr. Gregg, was even there, among the spectators. Somewhere. He'd had a visit from a certain branch of the government and been told to mind his manners. Now? I had no idea what he had planned. Nor did I care.

He was nobody now.

Dominique followed. She'd had the opportunity to sign hundreds of new clients. For some reason she'd turned them all down. When I asked her about it, she just smiled and told me I'd find out eventually. She was enjoying being mysterious, so I didn't push.

My friends made it to the front and took their places off to one side. There, looking like the most handsome, amazing, stunning man—male—to ever live, was Tane.

The music changed. Everyone rose to their feet. There was a long, pregnant pause, a silence that Chet had insisted would increase the suspense and anticipation of my appearance.

God, he was right. Even I was nervous now.

Until I took my first step and met Tane's gaze. He waited for me at the end of the petal-strewn carpet. He looked even more amazing than he had the night I met him. He looked like a prince, of course, but his jacket was black this time. The pattern of his family's mating cuffs was embroidered into his coat in gold and silver as well. Knee-high black boots, dark black pants. Once again his shoulders were adorned with gold, and gold buttons lined the front of the jacket. With his brown hair and intense eyes, he literally looked good enough to eat, which I planned to do later. Maybe not actually devour, but definitely sample. Taste. Lick. Suck. Nibble. Kiss. Lots and lots of kissing. That was a very important element of the Tane Experience.

Personal opinion, of course, because he was mine and I didn't share.

Chet and I took our time, as we had rehearsed, moving slowly toward my mate as he stood, impatience growing on his brow.

"We'd better hurry up," I whispered.

"No way, sweetheart. Not a chance."

Chet made him wait. Made the whole world wait. When I arrived, Tane leaned down and kissed me. And kissed me. I never wanted him to stop.

Chet cleared his throat. "Tane, it's not time for that yet." With a grin completely lacking in remorse, Chet grinned and placed my hand in Tane's. We walked to the officiant together. We'd obtained a marriage license. Everything was official. Real.

We said our vows. When he spoke, Tane repeated his twice. Once as himself, and once as his beast.

The big brute had the nerve to kiss me, too.

We didn't need wedding rings. Instead we'd asked an Atlan jeweler to create a special adornment that would attach to both of our mating cuffs. Since it was my wedding—and a human tradition—I'd been the one to choose what we added to our cuffs. I'd chosen a locket built into the left wrist. Inside mine was a holographic image of Tane. My likeness was inside his. They were small but beautiful, and I'd always have him with me now.

He would always be with me. Next to me. Protecting

me. Loving me. Listening to me. Caring. Waiting for me. *Wanting me.* Always. Until death do us part.

"I now pronounce you Atlan and wife." The man performing the ceremony had done so with a flourish, no doubt for the cameras.

I grabbed my beast and kissed him. Hard. With everything in me. Every ounce of love and life and promise I could give him. Because he was mine.

And I was his.

Forever.

EPILOGUE

E *lena, Interstellar Brides Processing Center, Miami*

I'D BEEN A HAPPILY married woman for about a month. Chet had recorded and photographed and interviewed both Tane and myself to death. Literally. I was exhausted.

Which was one of the reasons I was so excited to begin my new life. We were transporting to The Colony. Saying goodbye to Abby and Dominique had turned out to be more difficult than I'd anticipated. So they were both here with me, staring at the transport pad as Tane spoke to the alien behind the control panel.

I wondered if his name was Scotty.

"Well, I guess this is it?" Abby pulled me into a bear hug and squeezed so hard I had trouble breathing.

"You'll be okay, Abby. You'll be great. You're famous now. Really, really famous. I'm so proud of you." Abby had gained millions of followers on her social media accounts after the ball and the wedding. She was on equal footing with Chet in the celebrity world, and that was saying something. "You can make a ton of money on your own and never have to worry about your dad again. He won't be able to control you now."

"I know. But I thought I would be happier when I got this big. Instead it's kind of..."

"Lonely?" Dominique finished our young friend's sentence for her.

"Yes. No one gives a shit what I actually care about or need in my life. It's like I'm the ripe cherry and everyone wants to take a bite."

Dominique crossed her arms over her chest and raised her brows. "A cherry? Really? Was that the only fruit you could think of?"

Abby laughed. "Of course not."

We all giggled like silly little girls and pulled one another into a circle hug.

"I'm going to miss you like crazy," I said.

"Same," said Abby.

Dominique took a deep breath and looked at each of us for a long moment. "I guess now is as good a time as any to tell you."

"Tell us what?" I asked.

"I volunteered to be a bride. And I requested The Colony." Dominique squealed. "I'm going to be on The Colony with you!"

"What?" Shock flooded me, followed by joy. Disbelief. "Why?"

Dominique looked over her shoulder at Tane and

jerked her head in his direction. "Duh. Hot aliens. I'll take an Atlan if that's what I get, but I'm really hoping for a pair of those sexy Prillons."

"Holy shit, you're serious." I stepped back to look her in the eye, my arm still around Abby.

"As a heart attack."

"When do you go?"

"In about ten minutes." Warden Egara walked into the room and smiled at me. "That's if I can find a break in the schedule. Since you and Tane and your sex tape, the number of brides coming in has more than tripled."

Abby grinned. "No doubt. Every single lady out there wants a hot piece of alien sex god for herself."

My face was on fire. Had to be. "I'm glad I could help."

Warden Egara nodded and handed a tablet to Abby. "Finish this form and I'll add you to the schedule, dear."

"What?" I screeched.

Tane returned to me at that moment, his arm coming around me at once. "What's wrong?"

"I'm going to volunteer to be a bride." Abby pointed at Dominique. "And so is she."

My big beast looked confused. "Why is this a bad thing?"

I wiped tears from my cheeks. "It's not. Are you going to The Colony, too?" I asked Abby.

She shook her head. "I could. I thought about it. But I want to do this for me, you know? I want the best possible match, the ninety-nine percent, perfect-for-me match."

"Good for you. You deserve to be happy." Dominique pulled Abby into a hug. "And maybe we'll see you on The Colony anyway. You never know."

"You never know," Abby agreed.

Content, happy for my friends, and in love with my beast, I hugged my friends, said goodbye, and walked to the transport pad to start my new life.

My wonderful, sexy, adventurous new life with my very own Beast Charming.

A SPECIAL THANK YOU TO MY READERS...

Want more? I've got *hidden* bonus content on my web site *exclusively* for those on my mailing list.

If you are already on my email list, you don't need to do a thing! Simply scroll to the bottom of my newsletter emails and click on the *super-secret* link.

Not a member? What are you waiting for? In addition to ALL of my bonus content (great new stuff will be added regularly) you will be the first to hear about my newest release the second it hits the stores—AND you will get a free book as a special welcome gift.

Sign up now! http://freescifiromance.com

FIND YOUR INTERSTELLAR MATCH!

YOUR mate is out there. Take the test today and discover your perfect match. Are you ready for a sexy alien mate (or two)?

VOLUNTEER NOW!

interstellarbridesprogram.com

DO YOU LOVE AUDIOBOOKS?

Grace Goodwin's books are now available as
audiobooks...everywhere.

LET'S TALK!

Interested in joining my **Sci-Fi Squad**? Meet new like-minded sci-fi romance fanatics and chat with Grace! Get excerpts, cover reveals and sneak peeks before anyone else. Be part of a private Facebook group that shares pictures and fun news! Join here:

https://www.facebook.com/groups/scifisquad/

Want to talk about Grace Goodwin books with others? Join the **SPOILER ROOM** and spoil away! Your GG BFFs are waiting! (And so is Grace) Join here:

https://www.facebook.com/groups/ggspoilerroom/

GET A FREE BOOK!

JOIN MY MAILING LIST TO BE THE FIRST TO KNOW OF NEW RELEASES, FREE BOOKS, SPECIAL PRICES AND OTHER AUTHOR GIVEAWAYS.

http://freescifiromance.com

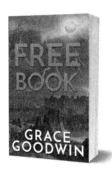

ALSO BY GRACE GOODWIN

Surprise Mates

Interstellar Brides® Program: The Colony

Surrender to the Cyborgs

Mated to the Cyborgs

Cyborg Seduction

Her Cyborg Beast

Cyborg Fever

Rogue Cyborg

Cyborg's Secret Baby

Her Cyborg Warriors

Claimed by the Cyborgs

The Colony Boxed Set 1

The Colony Boxed Set 2

The Colony Boxed Set 3

Interstellar Brides® Program: The Virgins

The Alien's Mate

His Virgin Mate

Claiming His Virgin

His Virgin Bride

His Virgin Princess

The Virgins - Complete Boxed Set

Interstellar Brides® Program: Ascension Saga

Ascension Saga, book 1

Ascension Saga, book 2

Ascension Saga, book 3

Trinity: Ascension Saga - Volume 1

Ascension Saga, book 4

Ascension Saga, book 5

Ascension Saga, book 6

Faith: Ascension Saga - Volume 2

Ascension Saga, book 7

Ascension Saga, book 8

Ascension Saga, book 9

Destiny: Ascension Saga - Volume 3

Interstellar Brides® Program: The Beasts

Bachelor Beast

Maid for the Beast

Beauty and the Beast

The Beasts Boxed Set

Big Bad Beast

Beast Charming

Bargain with a Beast

Starfighter Training Academy

The First Starfighter

Starfighter Command

Elite Starfighter

Starfighter Training Academy Boxed Set

Other Books

Dragon Chains

Their Conquered Bride

Wild Wolf Claiming: A Howl's Romance

ABOUT GRACE

Grace Goodwin is a USA Today and international bestselling author of Sci-Fi and Paranormal romance with over a million books sold. Grace's titles are available worldwide on all retailers, in multiple languages, and in ebook, print, audio and other reading App formats.

Grace is a full-time writer whose earliest movie memories are of Luke Skywalker, Han Solo, and real, working light sabers. (Still waiting for Santa to come through on that one.) Now Grace writes sexy-as-hell sci-fi romance six days a week. In her spare time, she reads, watches campy sci-fi and enjoys spending time with family and friends. No matter where she is, there is always a part of her dreaming up new worlds and exciting characters for her next book.

Grace loves to chat with readers and can frequently be found lurking in her Facebook groups. Interested in joining her **Sci-Fi Squad**? Meet new like-minded sci-fi romance fanatics and chat with Grace! Get excerpts, cover reveals and sneak peeks before anyone else. Join here: https://www.facebook.com/groups/scifisquad/

Want to talk about Grace Goodwin books with others? Join the **SPOILER ROOM** and spoil away! Your GG BFFs are waiting! (And so is Grace) Join here:

https://www.facebook.com/groups/ggspoilerroom/

Printed in Great Britain
by Amazon